The Tangled Web

The Tangled Web

Hazel Ro

www.urbanbooks.net

Urban Books, LLC
300 Farmingdale Road, N.Y.-Route 109
Farmingdale, NY 11735

The Tangled Web

ISBN 13: 978-1-64556-522-2
Ebook ISBN: 978-1-64556-523-9

First Trade Paperback Printing September 2023
Printed in the United States of America

10 9 8 7 6 5 4 3 2 1

Distributed by Kensington Publishing Corp.
Submit Orders to:
Customer Service
400 Hahn Road
Westminster, MD 21157-4627
Phone: 1-800-733-3000
Fax: 1-800-659-2436

Acknowledgments

Grateful is the only word I can use to describe the way I feel at this very moment in writing my acknowledgments. First and foremost, I must always thank my Heavenly Father. He is the one who gave me the gift of writing, gave me a very vivid imagination full of creativity, as well as the dedication to complete my third novel in the past three years. I am overwhelmed with gratitude to be on this journey, and I am truly indebted to be able to touch a small part of the hearts and lives of those that come in contact with my books. Thank you, God, for choosing me and trusting me with this.

Then, it goes without saying that I must thank everyone with Urban Books, from Carl Weber to Martha Weber, Jasmine Weber, Karen, and anyone else behind the scenes. I thank you all from the bottom of my heart for working with me, and your patience and dedication in getting my novels to where they need to be. You have all become like a family to me, and I would not want to work with any other publishing company. I especially thank my editor for this book. Alanna Boutin, I appreciate your words of encouragement and your commitment to making this novel its best.

Then, as always, a heartfelt thanks goes to my family, friends, and each and every one of my new book friends. I can only hope that I have once again created a quality read that captures your hearts, minds, souls, and imaginations. I do this solely for you, so with that, I simply say thank you!

Prelude

Mariah

My eyes popped open, and my back shot up straight in our fifteenth-century European canopy-style bed. As I felt around on the other side of it, my mind started to wander, and my heart raced in a panic when his solid, muscular frame was nowhere to be found. Then quickly, I slid my feet into my slippers while wrapping my black satin robe around my body.

"Malcolm? Malcolm?" I called out as I began to walk from room to room, looking for any signs of life. There was no response. Immediately, I felt a chill shoot straight through my body, leaving goose bumps down my arms. Something was odd, extremely odd, about the night, but for the life of me, I couldn't seem to put my finger on it. Not to mention the dream I'd experienced had me frantic. I couldn't trace all the details of it, but the last thing I recalled was his body lying on the other side of our bed—bloody and lifeless.

As I continued to check the rooms in the house, I felt a cold dampness throughout it, and all I could hear was the roar from the waves tossing and crashing against the rocks outside. The sound reminded me of all those years ago when we first married and why I was so against purchasing this home in Myrtle Beach, South Carolina. Malcolm had gotten it as my wedding gift. I could still remember his excitement like it was yesterday from his anticipation of surprising me. It was the very day we'd returned from our honeymoon in Dubai. All I wanted was to get back and begin our lives as husband and wife, quiet and simple. Yet, Malcolm, however, was the full-blown extrovert that I wasn't. He needed everyone to see from our lifestyle, the cars we drove, and especially the home we lived in that we were very well off financially. With that said, that day, he'd blindfolded me and led me into this 24,000-square-foot luxury oceanfront home. At first glance, it was absolutely breathtaking, but all I felt was pure anxiety from thinking about how close we'd be to the water.

Truth be told, my fear came from an incident involving my younger brother around the age of 7. My parents and I vowed never to talk about it after the accident. It was much too painful to even think about, which was mainly why I hadn't shared it with Malcolm all these years. Anyway, I begged and pleaded with him for us to find a much smaller condo and maybe grow into a home of this magnitude later when we started having children. But his pride and ego wouldn't let him relent. He said he'd worked too hard to have the life he'd always dreamed of for him and his wife, and marrying me had sealed the deal. Of course, I'd given in, but still, almost ten years later, my soul hadn't settled with living this close to the ocean.

As I reached our living room, my eyes caught a quick glimpse of the display on our sixty-four-inch flat-screen TV. It was at that moment that I realized why I felt so unsettled. Malcolm had never made it a habit to come home after midnight, and the display on the screen read ten minutes after one in the morning. Although I didn't want to assume the worst, my gut told me that either something was completely wrong or that his lateness had to do with *her*.

Ever since I'd brought that woman into our lives, it seemed as if Malcolm was changing into someone I didn't know, and I'd been regretting this whole ordeal. He'd been telling me it was all in my head, but something wasn't adding up about her or their relationship. I hadn't said much to Malcolm about it for fear of seeming insecure, but with her holding all the right cards in her hands, it was a no-brainer. Not to mention her beauty alone was enough to make any man go crazy.

What on earth did you do, Mariah? Why did you ever bring this woman into our lives? I asked myself, finally making it to our kitchen. Grabbing the wineglass I'd used earlier in the evening from the sink, I rinsed it out and poured the remaining contents of the wine bottle into it. Then leaning up against our white marble-topped kitchen island, I contemplated things further.

All I wanted was to give you a son, Malcolm, and now, because of it, our marriage might be destroyed. All at once, I started thinking of my next move, whether to call *her* directly and tell her to put my husband on the phone or go to her home to catch both of them red-handed. Either way, he'd be shocked because it was unlike anything I'd ever done. But I felt it was needed to put my mind at ease.

Pulling out another bottle of wine, I attempted to fill myself with enough liquid courage to do the latter. However, my practical side advised against it. Instead, with my wineglass in hand, I walked back into the living room, where I'd left my cell phone on the coffee table.

"All right, Mariah, are you *really* going to do this?" I questioned my alter ego. Then before I knew it, I downed the last bit of wine . . . and dialed her number.

"Hello?" She answered on the first ring in a soft and muffled tone. It was strange because I knew exactly what I wanted to say before I called, but having her on the phone suddenly made my mind blank.

"Hello? Mariah?" She called my name, I'm sure from seeing my number on display.

"Uh, yes, is Malcolm—"

Before I could finish, someone rang the doorbell several times in quick succession. Then, looking out the glass doors that led from our family room to the patio, I could see blue and red lights flashing from several cars.

What are the police doing here? I wondered, praying it had nothing to do with my uneasiness about my husband. "Uh, hold on for just a sec. I need to get this." As I slowly cracked the door open, the tall, stocky gentleman quickly flashed his badge.

"I'm sorry to come to your home so late, ma'am, but are you the wife of Mr. Malcolm Carter?"

Pulling the door open farther, I almost hesitated to answer. "Uh, yes, Officer, yes, I am. But what is this about? Is something wrong?"

"Mrs. Carter, I am Detective Wilson, and this is Detective Murphy. I hate having to tell you this, but—"

"But what?" I cut him off while recalling my dream. "What's going on?"

"Ma'am, I'm sorry, but there's been an accident involving your husband, and he's . . ."

At that very moment, I honestly didn't hear another word he said. All I can remember is my cell phone dropping from my hand and hitting the floor as I fell into the detective's arms in agony.

Chapter 1

Malcolm

I'd been craving her dark chocolate skin all week, and now, here we were at our regular meeting spot. I couldn't have been happier, although my mind kept reminding me that this would be our last time together. Of course, not that I truly wanted it to be, but that it *had* to be. As I lay there for at least ten minutes, I continually tried to think of ways that things could be different, but being honest with myself, I knew they simply couldn't. This thing between us had gone on long enough. It had to end before my whole world crashed down on me and I lost everything. As I thought about how to address things, I suddenly heard her angelic voice call out to me.

"Are you ready for me, Mr. Malcolm Carter?" she asked, standing in the doorway of the master bath.

As my eyes glided up and down her body from head to toe, I thought she was the sexiest woman that walked the face of the earth. Eva and I went back as far as our high school days. Back then, she was extremely shy, bashful, and completely insecure about her looks. She always kept to herself with her head tucked away in some book. She was the total opposite of me, who was more like the school's socialite. I was the star running back, the class president, and pretty much the life and soul of every party. Yet, in my eyes, there was something very intriguing about Eva. I loved how intelligent she was and the way she didn't hide it, either.

She was most confident in class, sometimes to the point where she challenged the teachers on their own theories. That alone fascinated me because she wasn't like all the other shallow and clueless girls we grew up with. Plus, although no one else could see it, I was mesmerized by her natural beauty. Eva didn't need a face full of makeup or a head filled with weave. Eva was just different, and I liked it. And although it took some time for her to grow into her looks and develop her confidence, she was still amazing to me, even in all her awkwardness.

She and I secretly became each other's best friends during our last couple of years of high school. We talked all the time about anything and everything or even nothing at all. Sometimes, we would walk to school together; other times, we'd meet up afterward.

Eva had become my listening ear to things I couldn't share with anyone else. I'd confided in her about my family issues, dreams, hopes, fears, and so much more. She pretty much did the same. However, even back then, I could tell she had her reservations. Eva would only go so far with what she revealed to me.

Our bond was as tight as two people could be. The only ones that knew about us were us. There was no way I could have let anyone discover how close I had become to her. I wasn't ashamed of Eva, but she was simply from a different world than me. My family and friends had wealth and prestige, while hers didn't. Eva had come from a single-parent home without her father around and with her mother struggling to make ends meet, while my family, on the other hand, gave money to not-so-well-off families like hers as a tax write-off.

And then there were my friends, like my best friend, Cedric. He would have never understood my infatuation with a girl like Eva because of the prettier and more popular girls I had chasing after me. In fact, that was probably one of the very reasons he and I had become close friends. Cedric was quieter and shy, but when girls saw him with me, it gave him the confidence he lacked. I would let him date the girls I wasn't so interested in, except for Eva. To this very day, neither he nor anyone else ever knew about us.

Anyway, my friendship with Eva was short-lived once I went to college, and we lost touch. At least, that was until I came back home for a visit. We bumped into each other at a gathering of mutual friends, and I couldn't seem to pull myself away from her. Little Eva had all grown up, and just as I'd imagined, she was absolutely breathtaking, just like now as she stood before me.

Her skin wasn't just dark but more of a midnight tone. It was moist and without any blemishes at all. She stood about five foot eight, not too small or overly thick. Her body was perfectly proportioned with curves in all the right places. Her eyes were a smoldering dark brown, with half-moon-like crests sculpted into her cheekbones. She had a button nose that sat atop her big puffy, pouting lips that were always pillow soft. Her teeth were perfect, sparkling white that adorned her radiant smile. And her hair was natural, with waves of midnight black cascading over her shoulders without any chemicals. There she stood in a white baby doll bra and panty set and white six-inch heels while my eyes took in every inch of her. Long ago, I started calling her "my Eve" instead of Eva because she was my temptress in our own little secret garden. Suddenly, my manhood jumped for joy at the thought of what would take place.

"Hell yes, Eve. Yes, yes, yes, baby, I am ready for you."

Slowly, she glided over to the bed, climbed in, and straddled her thick thighs over my lower portion, swallowing all of me. I let out an enormous groan as soon as he connected with her moistness, expressing my overwhelming satisfaction. Then without any hesitation, she began riding him as my large hands gripped her bubble-like cheeks, holding on for dear life. I could tell that it was what we both needed and wanted at that very moment.

After a few minutes of her doing her thing on top of me, I damn near could have exploded that very second. But not wanting to seem like a "minute man," I decided to take control and flipped her over on her back.

"Oh, Malcolm," she called out in her seductive tone, and that was when I really began to handle my business. I threw her legs over my shoulders so my strokes would hit deeper. And I assumed I was doing my job when her moans and groans became louder and more intense. We were both in pure ecstasy, and for the life of me, I couldn't imagine that moment ever ending.

"Oooh, don't stop, Malcolm. Please, baby, don't stop," she bellowed, her fingernails sinking deeper into my back. I tried my best to oblige her and hold back my climax. My lips met hers, and our tongues floated in slow motion with each other's until we both felt the inevitable.

"I'm coming, baby, I'm coming," she screamed while her legs shook uncontrollably, and I finally felt my release in sight.

"Oooh, baby, it's coming," I yelled, and at once, I felt her legs grip my waist like a sumo wrestler. I pushed myself as far as I could inside her warmth, letting go of every bit of me. Then a second after and feeling totally depleted, I rolled over on my back, allowing us both to catch our breath. Before I could close my eyes and drift into never-never land, I felt her hand slowly creeping up my chest.

"Damn, baby, I wish we could have this all the time," she whispered softly.

"Yeah, me too," I said, pulling her closer and kissing her forehead.

"So, why can't we, Malcolm? I mean, if we both feel the same, then why can't we finally be together? All the time."

"Eva, please don't start. You already know the answer to that. Besides, that's kind of what we need to talk about anyway," I reluctantly said while freeing her from my arms and putting a little space between us. Then propping my head on one hand, I tried to look into her eyes so that she could understand the seriousness of the situation. But as I did, I could immediately see the pain beginning to build within them. I could also see the millions of questions forming in the back of her mind, especially when they all came spilling out one after the other, not giving me a chance to utter a single word.

"What do you mean, that's what we need to talk about? Talk about *what,* Malcolm? And why are things suddenly feeling so awkward and final between us?"

"Well . . ." I sat up on the side of the bed, turning my back to her. "Because this has to be our last time together, Eva. We just can't do this anymore. *I* can't do this anymore."

"What? Why? Is it because of *her?* A woman that you're not even in love with and never have been?" she yelled behind me. But hearing her words made me snap. Before I knew it, I turned around, shooting a mean glance directly at her.

"Listen!" I raised my voice. "Don't you ever let me hear those words come from your mouth again. Do you hear me, Eva? *Ever.*"

"All right, all right, I hear you, Malcolm, but I need you to hear me too," she shot back. "We've been together for years, ever since you returned home from college.

And you told me that you would get rid of her. You said you just needed to find the right time to do it, and then it would be all about us. You said you no longer cared about what your family or friends thought because you loved me and not her. Well, I've waited, with excuse after excuse and one promise after the next. So, what happened, Malcolm? What happened to the promises you made to me?"

"What happened was I did fall in love with her, okay? And I'm sorry, Eva. I don't even know when it happened, but the truth is, it happened. And, well, I don't want to risk everything that I have in my marriage for—"

She cut me off. "For what? For *me?* You don't want to risk it all for me is what you're saying, right?" She hopped out of bed, went over to the sofa, and began sliding on her jeans and top. "Your money, wealth, influence, and good name are far too much to lose for the unsuccessful, penniless woman you love. Well, don't worry. I get it, Malcolm."

I ran over and grabbed her, turning her toward me. "Look, that's not what I meant. It's just that we both knew how different we were, how different our lives and backgrounds were from the beginning. And we also knew that we couldn't go on with this forever. And I need to stop this now before someone truly gets hurt."

"Wow, well, that's a little too damn late, Malcolm Carter, because someone *is* hurt. *I* am hurt—*deeply* hurt—not that it seems like you care, though. But you know what? I'm not going to give you the satisfaction of being one of those women whimpering, crying, and chasing after you, begging you to stay. You should already know that that's not me and will never be. So, go ahead and run to your wife and play the good ol' faithful husband you haven't been for the past nine years. And don't you *ever* dial my number again." She snatched away from me, picked up her pumps and bag, and headed toward the door.

"Eva, wait, please. Baby, it wasn't supposed to end like this. Please, come back," I begged and pleaded, chasing her out the door, forgetting I was completely naked. But none of it helped anyway. She simply walked out without another word or looking in my direction. I stood there, confused about if I'd done the right thing . . . until the door to the room next to mine opened.

"What's all the noise out here—?" the woman asked until her words halted, and her eyes roamed up and down my body before they focused directly on my main attraction. "Well, damn."

"I'm-I'm sorry, ma'am. I didn't mean to disturb you," I said, stuttering while trying to cover myself with my hands.

"It's no disturbance at all, sir, and actually, you're welcome to come in and join me if you'd like. I'm all alone."

"Uh, I'm sorry, ma'am, but I can't." I started walking back into the room as fast as I could and closed the door behind me.

Leaning my back against the door and thinking of what had just happened with Eva, I felt horrible. Yet, I knew it was something that needed to be done. In fact, maybe I should have done it long ago. The truth was, I didn't want to lose everything I'd built with Mariah, not my home, cars, and especially not my millions. I knew that although I loved what Eva and I shared, if I walked away from my marriage for her, I'd more than likely walk away with nothing. Any judge would award Mariah pretty much everything, especially if she ever learned of my affair. Anyway, I no longer had time to dwell on things with Mariah because my cell phone began to play my favorite tune, just like clockwork. I went to the nightstand and cleared my throat, hoping to sound as normal and upbeat as possible.

"Hey, sweetie, I'll be home in a bit, all right?" I answered on the first ring.

"Okay, honey. Oh, and do you mind stopping by the cleaners on your way? I didn't get a chance to swing by there today and pick up our clothes."

"Of course, sure thing, babe."

"Thank you, my love, and, Malcolm, I love you."

"I . . . I love you too, sweetheart. I really do."

Mariah and I never got off the phone or left each other without saying I love you. Hopefully, from this time forward, I could say it and make an effort to mean it too. After hanging up, it was clear to me that I had done the right thing by letting go of Eva, no matter how much it hurt either of us.

Chapter 2

Mariah

I loved hearing those three words come from his mouth every day.

"Baby, I'm home."

Shutting off the water in our master bathroom, I stepped out and wrapped a towel around my body. I heard his footsteps approaching our kitchen before heading to our master suite. My nipples immediately stood at attention, just at the mere thought of my husband. It amazed me how Malcolm still had that kind of effect on me after all these years. I loved and adored everything about him, the good and the not-so-good. He was exactly the type of man I'd prayed to spend my life with, and God had answered my prayers through a simple chance meeting.

It was my best friend Crystal's twenty-first birthday and graduation party. Her parents had gone all out, practically giving her the pool party of the century. Everyone who was anyone was there, and they surprised her with her favorite male singing group and even let all of us have a glass of champagne when the clock struck midnight. It was a party that all our friends talked about for quite a long time, maybe even still to this very day. However, Crystal couldn't get into the swing of it all because she thought her high school sweetheart, Cedric, had forgotten all about her birthday. She hadn't heard from him that entire day until he showed up almost two hours late to the party, him and his best friend, Malcolm. Needless to say, her whole attitude changed the second she laid eyes on him and the huge gift box in his hands.

They ended up leaving Malcolm and me alone while they snuck to make out in her bedroom. It was Malcolm's and my first meeting, but from that night forward, we seemed inseparable. He and I dated for around four years before he asked for my hand in marriage, and I happily obliged, and now we are living happily-ever-after just like in a fairy tale.

A few seconds later, he walked into the bedroom with long-stemmed red roses in his hand. My eyes lit up like they did every time I saw my husband. He was perfect to me in every single way. He stood tall with a solid, muscular frame. His skin was caramel brown, and all his features were chiseled to perfection. His style was always polished and refined, and everything about him seemed regal and grand. Malcolm was truly any woman's dream, and I was glad he was mine.

"Hey, baby, how are you?"

"Great now that I'm home with you," he said, laying the roses on the bed and pulling my body close to his. Instantly his lips slowly caressed mine as his tongue entered my mouth. My tongue intermingled with his in a slow and steady motion before I felt my towel sliding off and hitting the floor. His large hands immediately cuffed my breasts, and he massaged my nipples. Then his kisses started to get stronger as I felt his manhood rising and pressing against me.

"Whoa, whoa, soldier," I said, struggling to pull away from him and not give in to my desires. "Sweetie, you know we can't do that tonight. We need to get dressed and hurry up and leave."

"Leave? To go where?" he questioned with his face all frowned.

"Honey, don't you remember? We told Crystal and Cedric we'd come by tonight for dinner and to see Cedric Junior. I haven't seen him since they brought him home from the hospital, and I'm dying to kiss his sweet little face."

"Damn, baby, do we really have to do that tonight?" He crawled out of his suit jacket and walked toward the kitchen. "I mean, can't we reschedule? I'm beat, and all I wanted was a quiet evening here with you. I even brought home some takeout and thought we would share a nice dinner by the water. Doesn't that sound better?" he asked, finally making it to the kitchen with me trailing right behind him.

"That would sound great any other time, Malcolm, but not tonight. We're not going to reschedule. I promised Crystal we were coming, and besides, as I said, it would be our first time seeing the baby since they brought him home. Don't you want to see him and hold him too? I mean, we *are* his godparents."

He pulled the takeout from the bag and set it on the island. Then he rinsed a glass from the dishwasher and poured himself a shot of bourbon. "Listen, sweetie, I'm sure if I call Ced that he'll be cool with us rescheduling for another time. Besides, although I would love to see the baby, I'm just not in the mood for your friend to give me dirty looks and mumble hateful things under her breath all night, all right? We both know that she doesn't like me for whatever reason, and the feeling is about to become mutual." He headed right back to our bedroom while I stayed on his heels, praying he'd change his whole attitude. Once there, he sat on the edge of the bed and began removing his shoes. I sat beside him and began massaging his back to ease his tension.

"Honey, don't you think it's about time you and Crystal buried whatever hatchet you have between you two?" I suddenly noticed a scent on his clothing that wasn't mine and was a lot sweeter than his cologne.

"Listen, I don't have the issue. It's her, and you know it," he said, turning around to face me, and kissed me again. However, that time I couldn't return the sentiment because of the fragrance that had consumed my thoughts.

"Look, I just don't want to argue about going to Crystal and Ced's, okay? We made a promise to our friends, and plus, I just want to get out of the house tonight." I stopped massaging his back and walked over to my vanity table, trying to distance myself from that scent. But it became stronger when he got up, gripped my waist from behind, and set his chin on my shoulder.

"All right, baby, all right. If going will put you in a better mood, then we'll go, and I guess I'll try to play nice with your friend all night. I'm sorry I upset you."

He kissed my cheek but released his embrace the second he felt his phone buzzing in his pants. My eyes followed him closely as he answered while walking into the bathroom and closing the door behind him. I hadn't wanted to admit it, but tonight wasn't the first night I'd smelled that scent. I was positive I'd smelled it consistently for the past few months. However, it could have been there long before, and I hadn't paid much attention to it. But just like when I began recognizing it, I noticed how he'd come home in an extremely good mood with flowers or a gift for me.

All at once, I felt like someone had stuck a pin in me and released all the air within. I couldn't breathe at the thought of my husband being with another woman. As far as I knew, he'd never once cheated on me. In fact, let him tell it, he'd never even looked in another woman's direction. So, of course, I had no reason not to believe him, either, but his recent behavior was beginning to make me a bit concerned.

As much as I didn't want to assume anything negative, his actions seemed odd and a little suspicious. First, whenever his phone rang, he always had to take the call in a separate room from me. Then every time I called his office around lunchtime every day, he was always tied up in a meeting. And then there was this perfume all over his clothing. I'd never once told him about any of my suspicions, but I wasn't sure how much longer I could keep quiet.

"What's going on with you, Malcolm? Please don't let me find out you're cheating on me," I said to myself. "I'm not sure what I would do if I did."

Chapter 3

Eva

"What are you doing? What are all the back-to-back calls and texts about, Eva?" I could tell he was trying hard to whisper.

"Malcolm, I've been thinking about this since I left earlier. You have another think coming if you think that after all this time, you're just going to tell me it's over, and that's it."

"What the hell am I supposed to do? I mean, you know I'm married, and you know we couldn't keep this up forever. As I said earlier, I could lose everything I've worked so hard for, Eva, if she learned about my infidelity. And my gut has been feeling like she's becoming suspicious of my behavior. Besides, honestly, I know that she deserves way more than this. Plus, she's been mentioning having a family lately, and honestly, it's something I want too. So, how am I supposed to have all of that and continue sneaking around with you at the same time?"

His words felt like a huge slap in the face, and if I could have jumped through the phone, I surely would have.

"So, now you want a family with her—after you've told me for years that you would find a way to divorce her and be with me? Now you want to be one big happy family with her? Besides, what happened to you telling me that she's been struggling even to get pregnant, Malcolm? Has something changed that I don't know about?"

"Look, first of all, I won't let you lay some guilt trip on me about things. Now, did I make some promises? Yes, foolishly, I did, and I feel bad about all of it, but please understand that this is how it must be. Anyway, I can't get into all of this with you right now. You have to believe I feel horrible for this whole mess I've made, but my decision stands. We can't see each other anymore, and that's just how it has to be. I gotta go now."

"Malcolm, if you hang up this phone without settling things with me, I promise you'll live to regret it."

"Wait, are you *threatening* me?" he asked, his voice much more raised than before.

"The word 'threat' is so hostile, and, baby, you know I would never be that way with you. But trust me when I say it is a promise. Either you fix things with me and give me what you've always promised, or that sweet, precious little wife of yours will learn all about your dirty little secrets. Then we'll see how much she wants a family with you. Oh, by the way, Malcolm, does she know how much you like to have your ass—"

Before I knew it, he'd hung up on me, and I let out a huge, exasperated scream, throwing my phone at the wall. He had me much more outraged than he did earlier. I hated that I allowed him to have that much control over me, but the truth was he did. Although I'd always been the type of woman who knew I could have any man I wanted, my heart was with Malcolm Carter, and I refused to let go.

As I paced back and forth, trying to decide what to do next, I remembered that I truly held all the cards right in the pit of my belly. Going over to the mirror and pulling up my shirt, I started to examine if I'd begun showing any more than when I first went to the doctor. Although there was a slight bump, it wasn't very revealing to the natural eye. In other words, no one would know I was several weeks pregnant by just looking at me, including Malcolm.

With my hands touching my stomach, I began talking to the growing life inside me. "Everything is going to be just fine, little baby. Things might be a little crazy right now, but don't you worry. Your father will come around and give us the life I always hoped for and the life you and I deserve. Once he finds out about you, there will be no way he can talk about leaving us, especially not for that spoiled, senseless, infertile wife of his. Malcolm has always come through when I needed him most, and I promise that's never going to end . . . *ever.*"

I was speaking more to myself than the little fetus inside me, but I could tell he or she knew exactly what I was saying. All at once, my mind returned to the day I found out I was pregnant. I was so afraid and had no idea what to do. Part of me wanted to call Malcolm that day in hopes of him sharing in the joy of us having a baby, but the other half knew that neither my child nor I would possibly ever be accepted by him and his family. In fact, deep down, I had a gut feeling that Malcolm would suggest I abort it so that I wouldn't ruin his perfect image and life.

That moment took me back to all those years ago as a young girl, about to start my last year of high school without a clue if I even wanted to attend college. I'd gotten pregnant by the only boy I'd ever been with—Malcolm Carter. I was elated. Malcolm and I had only been together that one time, right before he went to college. Neither one of us ever meant for it to happen, but it did, and that night, we shared an innocent, beautiful display of our overall friendship.

We never spoke about it afterward, though. But then, finding out I was pregnant, I felt stuck between a rock and a hard place. There I was with a love child inside my womb, the one thing I knew would love me back unconditionally. But then, I knew I would have ruined

Malcolm's entire life at that time. I knew there was no way he would have left me all alone carrying his child while he went away to school. So, I did the only thing I knew to do. I sacrificed my child for his sake and mine. Our relationship had fizzled away anyway, so as much as my heart didn't agree, my mind said it was the right thing to do. At least, that was until we bumped into each other years later.

I'd laid eyes on Malcolm; he was just as handsome as he had been in high school, only more mature. My mind, heart, and every inch of my body desired the man so much that it suddenly made me reminisce about our high school years and our first time together. As I thought back, there was no way I could tell him that I'd kept the fact that I was pregnant by him and gotten an abortion. So, with that in mind, I didn't say a thing, and, of course, he hadn't either. In fact, I wasn't sure if he even remembered, so I left it as a distant and affectionate memory that I'd always have. However, every time we were together, I thought about our child and the type of father he would be.

I still wanted that with him, a family, that is. That was why I was determined not to let Malcolm's wife destroy my baby's or my future with him. He promised me that eventually he would leave Mariah and be with me, and now, I was going to make damn sure he kept his word. *I* would be the woman standing by his side in the end, with his one and only child as his legacy. We deserved his love and, more so, his fortune—not her—and I planned on that happening, even if that meant I had to get rid of her for good.

Chapter 4

Crystal

I was ecstatic to see my best friend, but that husband of hers was a whole other story. Just the thought of that man made my skin crawl. He was cocky and arrogant, and although I couldn't prove it, I had a gut feeling that he wasn't being faithful to Mariah. Of course, I never shared my theory with her. Instead, I hoped and prayed that one day his secrets would catch up with him or she would finally realize that she deserved someone so much better.

"Now, baby, you promise you'll play nice tonight, right?" Cedric asked while touching up his beard in our bathroom mirror.

"I said I wouldn't say anything out of the way to Malcolm, and I won't."

"Yeah, but I know you . . . saying that you won't say anything out of the way to him simply means you won't say anything at all to him."

"Well, that's the only way I can put up with the man," I said, turning my back to him. "Can you zip this up for me, please?"

"I just wish you would finally get over what happened all those years ago. So he made me late to your birthday party, but will you hold that against him forever?" he questioned as he zipped my dress and smacked me on the rear.

I looked at him without answering and went to the baby's room when I heard his cries from the baby monitor. Once I arrived, I picked up Cedric Junior, cradled him in my arms, and thought about what Cedric had said. If only my husband knew why I really hated Malcolm's guts, but I just couldn't force myself to say anything to anyone. I knew that if I did, Cedric would only say it was all in mind. Especially since Malcolm was practically like a big brother to him, and he worshiped the ground the man walked on. I knew he would take up for him until the end of time.

Then there was Mariah. Had I shared my suspicions with her, I was positive it would destroy our friendship forever. She would never hear anything negative about her perfect Malcolm from anyone, including me. So, I kept quiet all these years and prayed he never pushed me too far.

A few minutes later, I heard the doorbell buzzing. Looking down at Cedric Junior's little face, I prayed to make it through the night. "All right, little man, give Momma the strength she needs to not put her hands around your father's best friend's neck before this night ends."

Walking out of CJ's room, I found that Cedric had already let them in, and Malcolm and Mariah were removing their jackets.

"Oh my goodness, look at him. Auntie Mariah couldn't wait to see your little face," she said, walking toward me with her eyes lit up and immediately removing CJ from my arms. Then she kissed my cheek. "Oh yeah, I couldn't wait to see you either, girl."

"Yeah, yeah, I bet." I laughed and pushed her shoulder playfully.

"Good evening, Crystal. How have you been? We brought this for you guys." I heard his annoying voice inquire as he handed me a bottle of wine.

"Malcolm," was all that I could get out with a slight smirk on my face as I took the bottle from him. I mustered up everything inside of me to not haul off and crack him over the head with it.

"Uh, why don't we sit in the living room?" I heard Cedric say, knowing it was his way to lighten the tension already building in the room.

"Yes, please go and have a seat, and I'll grab the hors d'oeuvre and wineglasses from the kitchen to go with our gift."

"Girl, wait, let me come and help you."

"No, no, trust me, you are helping more than enough by keeping your godson quiet for me for a few seconds. I'm good."

They headed toward the living room while I entered the kitchen, where a platter of hors d'oeuvre sat on the island. Then I took four wineglasses from the wine cooler where I had them chilling, but a minute later, I was met by a very unwelcome visitor.

"Hey, I know you said you were good in here, Crystal, but I thought you might need some help anyway," Malcolm said in his usual smug tone.

"Malcolm, please, just go back in there with Mariah and Cedric. I said I was good."

"All right, but, um, I have one question before I leave."

"Go ahead. What's your question?" I continued to move around the kitchen while acting like I was paying attention to him.

"How long are we going to do this?"

"I don't think I know what you're talking about. Do what, Malcolm?" I asked while beginning to hate the fact that I had invited him over with Mariah.

"This whole 'I hate Malcolm, but I'm tolerating him' routine that you always do. Because honestly, Crystal, it's getting old, and I already told Mariah that I don't feel comfortable coming around if you always have this attitude with me."

"Look, I don't have an attitude, and I don't know what you're talking about, all right? So, please, just go, okay?"

"Not until you tell me what it is. I mean, there could only be one of two reasons you behave this way with me. Either you haven't gotten over what happened between us, or you still have a chip on your shoulder over the fact that I didn't choose you, and I let Cedric have you. So, which one is it?"

"Malcolm Carter, please don't flatter your damn self. I am very happy and in love with my husband, as I have always been. Besides, what happened with us was a huge mistake, and there's nothing about you that I would ever find desirable again," I said, yet knowing deep down there was only a small amount of truth to my words.

"Really? Is *that* what you've been telling yourself all these years because we both know how you felt in high school and even after. Hell, everyone knew, except for Cedric, that is."

"You cocky ass—"

"All right, all right." He cut me off, throwing his hands up as if finally conceding. "Then what is it?" He walked closer to me, taking the wineglasses from my hand. "Because it must be something. Do you still want me, Crystal?" he asked, standing right behind me. His cologne began to overwhelm me, and the warmth of his body consumed me. I immediately became moist and yearned to feel him inside of me.

"Please, Malcolm, don't do this."

"Well then, tell me what it is." I felt his hand creep up the side of my dress and inside my panties. "Because, to me, it feels like you still want me."

"Stop it," I said as I tried to snap out of the trance he'd had me in and make myself believe I really didn't like what was happening. Then I went to the other side of the island to place some distance between us and tried to cool off.

He smiled and laughed under his breath. "Then what is it, Crystal?" he asked again, staring dead into my eyes and then putting the same finger he'd just had inside of me in his mouth.

"You really want to know, huh, Malcolm?" I said, feeling I could no longer hold back. And maybe it was finally my time to let loose and let the chips fall where they may.

"Yeah, I really do. It's time we get whatever this is out in the open once and for all so that we can deal with it."

"Okay then, deal with this. I saw you, Malcolm Carter—the day before your and Mariah's wedding. I saw you and some woman outside the hotel where you, Cedric, and the other groomsmen stayed. You kissed her, and it wasn't just a mere peck on the cheek, either. You kissed her long and hard like you were madly in love with her."

"What?" He laughed under his breath again. "I don't know what you're talking about, Crystal, or what you *think* you saw, but it's not true." I could see the tension growing on his face immediately. And instead of the smug look he'd had a second ago, it looked like every vein would burst at any second.

"I know *exactly* what I saw, and my eyes weren't deceiving me." Picking up the tray of food, I tried to leave the kitchen, but he came around and grabbed me by the arm.

"Oh no, you don't get off that easy. First of all, what were *you* doing there? And if you saw me kissing another woman the day before my wedding, why didn't you say anything to Mariah?"

I yanked away from him and stared him dead in his eyes. "I went there, Malcolm, because of guilt. I felt like we needed to tell Mariah and Cedric what happened between us before you two got married. I just wanted it out in the open. But then I saw you with *her,* and I just left. Then after the wedding, I never said a word because if I did, it would have destroyed my best friend, and I wasn't about to do that to her, no matter how much I hate you. But please, don't push me now, Malcolm. Don't fuckin' push me because I *will* tell everything."

Picking up the tray of food again, I finally walked toward the living room as if our conversation had never happened. "Who's ready for some delicious hors d'oeuvre?" I went in with a huge smile.

"It's about time, girl. I thought I would have to come and look for you two," Mariah said, peering over my shoulder to look at her husband and ensure everything was all right.

"Oh, we were just catching up a bit, sweetie, right, Crystal?" he asked.

"Of course," I said as calmly as I could. However, Cedric must have sensed my overall displeasure.

"Baby, are you all right?"

"Of course, honey. I couldn't be happier right now with all the people I love in one room," I answered in between a fake smile and a quick glance in Malcolm's direction, struggling with whether I wanted to hate him or make love to him more at that very moment.

"Crystal, CJ is the cutest little baby I've ever seen," Mariah said, changing the climate in the room.

"Thank you, girl. I think so too," I said playfully.

"I've been sitting here looking at him, and I can't tell if he looks more like you or Cedric."

"Uh, we think he looks more like me right now, but I can see Cedric's features coming in every day."

"Well, either way, he is simply adorable, and I wish we could take him home with us."

"All right, be careful what you ask for because you two are his only set of godparents, and Cedric and I won't mind at all dropping him off to you." We all laughed as I watched Mariah hand CJ to Malcolm. Looking at them, I couldn't deny how comfortable and at ease Malcolm appeared with him. He was way more relaxed and secure than Cedric was. It was also amazing to see how content CJ was with him. With every other man that held him, he cried his little heart out, including Cedric and my father, but not Malcolm. CJ even had an adorable little smile across his face.

"Speaking of godparents, though, did you know Angie was pregnant?" Mariah asked me.

"Girl, stop. I didn't know that."

"Oh well, I'm sure she'll get around to telling you. She just said something to me yesterday."

"Hey, Malcolm, why don't we let the ladies catch up a little and have their woman talk while I show what I've done to my media room?" Cedric interrupted.

"Oh, okay, that's cool," he said, handing the baby back to Mariah.

Cedric grabbed the tray of food and his wineglass, while Malcolm took the bottle of wine and his glass and started walking toward the back of the house. The second they were out of the room, and I was no longer in his presence, I felt a huge sense of relief.

"All right, so spill it, girl. What happened in the kitchen with you and my husband?"

"Girl, nothing at all. He said he came to help with the hors d'oeuvre and wineglasses, and that was it."

"Crystal, I have known you long enough to know when you're lying, or something is bothering you. So, what is it with you and Malcolm? You know that you can tell me anything, right?" she asked, but I knew good and well I couldn't say what had truly happened.

"Look, maybe it's like he said in the kitchen. Maybe after all this time, I still haven't fully gotten over the fact that he made Cedric late to my birthday party."

"What? Is that *really* what it's been all these years? You almost had me thinking that you knew something about my husband that I didn't, and this has been about a party? Crystal, girl, you gotta let that go."

"I know, I know, and I will. I promise. But anyway, what's going on with you? How have *you* been?" I asked, admiring her turning CJ over and patting his back softly. Although she and Malcolm had no children, I knew in my heart that my friend would make the perfect mother one day, and I couldn't wait to see it.

"I've been good. I can't complain about anything. Work is good, my health is good, and my marriage is more than good. So, all is good in my world." She tried to crack a smile while saying the words, but I still didn't believe any of it.

"Really? Then why does it feel like there's something *you're* not telling me?" As I watched her eyes hang low, a minute or two passed before she started to speak again.

"Okay," she began, glancing toward Cedric's media room and lowering her voice. "Here's the thing. I'm feeling slightly unsettled about something from earlier tonight, and I'm still trying to process it."

"Well, maybe I can help. What is it? What's got you unsettled?" I started rubbing her leg because I could tell that whatever it was, it was truly bothering her.

"It's Malcolm, Crystal. For the past couple of months, I feel like he's been, I don't know . . . different."

"Different? Different how?"

"That's just it. I can't really put my finger on it. And maybe I'm just being paranoid or something because things have always been so perfect between us. But as of late, I feel as if he's always preoccupied when he's home.

And then there's the fact that he's always returning in an extremely good mood and bringing gifts, almost like he's trying to make up for something. Plus, I've smelled the same scent on his clothing daily. A woman's fragrance."

"And let me guess. You haven't said a word to him about anything?"

"Oh, of course not. I can't say anything to him about something I have no proof of. He would think I'm crazy, and as I said, it might just be all in my head anyway."

"But you and I both know it's not, Mariah. There is such a thing as women's intuition, which never steers us in the wrong direction."

"Look, I just don't want to go accusing my husband of anything I'm unsure about. That's not how we've ever done things in our marriage, and I'm not about to start now."

Her last comment almost felt like a jab at me because I'd always been far more outspoken than her. She knew I wouldn't dare allow Cedric to get away with half of the things she allows with Malcolm. Yet, I tried to ignore it and stay on the matter at hand.

"All right, so what do you do from here?"

"What can I do other than hope and pray that my paranoia is just that and that everything gets back to normal soon?"

I desperately wanted to tell my friend what I'd seen the night before their wedding and my theory that Malcolm was more than likely still being unfaithful. However, I wasn't sure if that very moment was the right time to do it. But the more I tried to keep quiet, something inside me kept pushing me to go ahead and let it out.

"Uh, Mariah, there's something I need to tell you. Something I know I should have said a long time ago."

"Is everything all right? What's wrong?"

Before I could collect my thoughts and get my words out, Cedric peeked in, and I cringed as if I'd been caught red-handed with my hand in the cookie jar.

"Uh, excuse me, ladies, but are we having dinner anytime soon because those hors d'oeuvre were demolished long ago."

"Uh, yeah, honey. Give me a second, okay?" I said, preparing to go into the kitchen. But the second he was out of eyesight, Mariah grabbed my arm.

"Crystal, wait. What was it that you were about to say to me?"

I took a quick second to think about whether I should share what I already knew about Malcolm and my current suspicions. However, my gut told me to hold off until I had more concrete evidence, which I planned to get.

"Oh, it was nothing, Mariah. I was only going to say that I'm sorry for how I've acted all this time with Malcolm. I truly apologize."

"You know it's okay, girl." She looked relieved by my response. "We both love you dearly, and I'm just glad it's finally all out in the open and done with."

We went into the kitchen, and a moment after, Cedric came in.

"It's going to be a few minutes to warm everything, honey, okay?" I said, immediately noticing that Malcolm wasn't with him.

"That's fine, babe. Malcolm had a call to take, and I just wanted to give him some privacy."

"I really should have taken his cell phone from him for the evening." Mariah giggled behind her statement. "I told him in the car that there would be absolutely no work tonight."

"Yeah, but you know your husband and my best friend. The only way he'll stop working is when he's in the grave.

Anyway, CJ looks like he's dozing off on your shoulder, so why don't I go and lay him down?"

"Oh, I'll do it, Cedric. He's used to his mommy tucking him in at night," I said playfully, but I had an ulterior motive behind my actions. I was well aware that we had a baby monitor in the media room, and I was positive I'd left it on earlier. I wanted to hear some of Malcolm's so-called business call.

Taking CJ from Mariah, I hurried back into his nursery and closed the door behind me. Then I quickly put his pacifier in his mouth so Malcolm wouldn't hear any of his baby noises once I turned up the monitor. Then slowly increasing the volume, I could hear his voice but could tell he was trying to whisper.

"Listen, I told you earlier that I was done with this and meant it. Now, do I love you? Of course, I do, but I love my wife more, and it's time that I do right by her."

For a few minutes, there was silence, and I almost started to get nervous that he knew I was listening . . . until he spoke again.

"What more do we have to talk about, Eva? All right, look, look, if it will stop you from calling and trying to mess up my night, then yes, I'll meet you . . . and no, not at our usual spot. We can meet at two o'clock tomorrow at the Starbucks on Tenth Street. I'll also tell you about the issue we might have with my wife's best friend. She's a little too nosy for her own good."

Turning down the volume, I'd heard more than an earful of what I needed to hear.

"Too nosy for my own good, huh? Well, we'll see about that, Malcolm, because I'm suddenly in the mood for an iced latte from Starbucks tomorrow around two. See you there."

Chapter 5

Mariah

The ride home from Crystal and Cedric's had been awkwardly quiet other than the constant vibrating of Malcolm's phone. In fact, my husband hadn't uttered a word at all during dinner or the rest of the evening, which was why we left earlier than planned. Something had his undivided attention, and I felt there was no better time than the present to find out what that was.

Pulling up to the house, he shut off the car and went inside without even opening my door. I walked in and entered the kitchen, where he'd already started pouring himself a drink.

"So, are we going to talk about what's bothering you all of a sudden?"

"What are you talking about, Mariah?"

"Honey, you haven't said two words since before dinner. It's like you've been in your own little world or something. What gives?"

"Baby, please don't start examining me, all right? It's late, I'm tired, and I just spent an entire evening trying to play nice with someone who hates me, and believe me, the feeling is starting to become mutual. And, please, don't ask me to do that again because I won't. Crystal is *your* friend, and Cedric is mine."

"Malcolm, first of all, we are both friends with Crystal. You've known her a lot longer than I have, and she and Cedric are why we're even together. Besides, she already told me everything that happened between you two in the kitchen tonight."

"What? What do you mean she told you everything? Everything like what? Because I'm telling you now that you can't believe *anything* your friend says. There's no telling what she might conjure up when it comes to me simply because she hates me," he let spill out, almost sounding a bit fearful and oversuspicious.

"Malcolm, all she said was that she was still upset with you all this time about making Cedric late to her birthday party, and she apologized. She even told me you two agreed to put it all behind you. So, can't you please do that? Can you at least try to forgive her for how she acted?"

"Uh, yeah, I forgot that we did talk about it." He started to sound relieved. "And, yeah, I guess I can try to forgive her too."

"Good, because all I want more than anything is for my husband and my best friend in the world to finally get along."

"I hear you. But, baby, why are we still talking about Crystal? Especially when all I want to do is finish what we started earlier and take my beautiful wife to our bedroom and make love to her like I've never made love to her before." He kissed the back of each of my hands, then my cheeks, and finally made his way to my lips in between his words. Although I still had a million questions regarding his behavior, I could never turn down my husband's advances.

Kissing him back, it seemed as if the whole notion of going to the bedroom had left just as quickly as it came.

Instead, he slowly unzipped my dress and watched it fall to the floor. Then he picked me up and set my rear atop the island. From there, he kissed his way up my legs until he came face-to-face with my moisture. I grabbed hold of his bald head as I felt his lips wrap around my clit. He licked and sucked for dear life, and I thought I would go crazy. Then before I knew it, he stopped, pulled me to the edge of the island, and I immediately felt his manhood enter inside me. For all these years, my husband had been the only man able to get me drenching wet, and tonight was no different. I could feel his nature rising more and more as every inch of him pounded in and out.

"Baby, please, don't stop," I pleaded with him, not wanting the pleasure to end. Malcolm obliged my request when he suddenly picked me up and put my back against our kitchen wall. His strength held me up as my body succumbed to each stroke. I knew I couldn't hold back any longer when my legs began to shake. My girlfriend had about all that she could take when, all at once, I felt her release.

"Oooh, baby, here it comes," I heard his baritone voice announce, and all at once, we both let go of everything we had pent up inside of us.

The next second, he carefully let my still, somewhat trembling legs down, and I slid down the wall to the floor in exhaustion. I watched his naked, muscular body go over to the sink and pour himself a glass of water. Then after gulping that down, he turned out the lights and walked back over to me with his hand outstretched. Pretty much helpless, I reached up to him, and he pulled me up, scooping my lower body into his arms, and carried me off to our bedroom.

Despite any feelings I had shared with Crystal earlier about the possibility of another woman, I did not doubt that Malcolm still loved and desired me. There was no way on earth our lovemaking could be as passionate and intense as it was if there were anyone else. With that in mind, I was going to sleep with a smile on my face and peace in my heart, something I hadn't done in a while.

Chapter 6

Malcolm

It seemed like the second I laid Mariah down and her head hit the pillow, she was out like a light. But before I crawled into bed beside her and grabbed some much-needed rest, I headed back down to the kitchen, where I'd left my cell phone in my pants pocket. It wasn't like I was expecting anyone to call, but I habitually checked it every morning for news, weather, and other trending topics. Not to mention, part of me feared Mariah being near my phone while I wasn't around. Of course, it wasn't like her to snoop or check it without my knowledge. But after the threat that Eva had made earlier, I simply couldn't take the chance of leaving it lying around for Mariah to come in contact with it.

Thinking of Eva, I couldn't wait to return to the room, close my eyes, and try to forget everything that had happened regarding her. In all the time I'd known her, she'd never once talked to me the way she had tonight, or better yet, had the *gall* to threaten me. That, in itself, left me a bit shaken. Although I was sure it would take some time, I prayed all evening that she would eventually come to grips with my decision sooner than later. I was optimistic that the quicker she did, she would find the love she'd always longed for with me. Eva was a beautiful, charismatic, and highly intelligent woman who would have men breaking down her door if she only gave them a chance. But then again, I only hoped that would be something I could handle if and when it did happen because truth be told, I loved her as much as she did me.

Another thing that had me feeling uneasy and rattled was the conversation with Crystal. I couldn't seem to take my mind away from what she had said in her kitchen. I had no idea she'd seen Eva and me together the night before my wedding. And although she hadn't said anything in all this time, something inside me told me she was waiting for the perfect moment to spill the beans to Mariah. That's exactly how much she hated me. If she couldn't have me, then she definitely didn't want any other woman to have me. In fact, I was positive that Crystal even hated the fact that I had married Mariah.

Although she continually tried to play the role of being the good wife to Cedric and best friend to Mariah, she and I both knew the truth. And whether or not she wanted to admit it, her feelings were clear from her behavior in the kitchen. She was wetter than the beachfront outside my home when I touched her. I knew Cedric could never have her that way, and she blamed me for that.

With that in mind, I had to think of a way to keep her mouth shut—for good. There was no way I could afford to lose my wife at this point because of either of those women, especially with all that we had invested. That was why I knew I had to end things with Eva. If Mariah ever found out about my affair, I could lose everything I'd worked so hard to get in life, and there was no way in hell I was about to let that happen.

Before taking my pants off the floor and returning upstairs, I poured myself another stiff drink. That, along with the sex Mariah and I had, was sure to put me out cold for some hours. However, as I stood there going over the day's events in my mind, I heard my cell phone vibrating.

Who in the world could be calling or texting me at this hour? I thought. I almost ignored it, but my gut told me exactly who it was. Moving quickly, I picked up my pants, yanked out my phone, and glanced at the screen. All at once, my heart started to race when my eyes read the words, Come to the door.

"What the fuck? What the hell is she up to now?" I questioned while sliding my pants on as quickly as I could.

Then hurrying to the front door, I prayed that this was some joke she was playing. But as I snatched open the door, I quickly found out that she was serious—dead serious. There she stood in a trench coat and black stilettos. I had to admit that she looked good enough to eat, and if I weren't furious, I probably would have done so in a heartbeat. But nothing, not even her looks, could change the fact that she showed up at my home unannounced, with my wife sleeping upstairs.

"What the hell are you doing here, Eva?" I said as best as I could, trying not to raise my voice but still letting her know I meant business.

"What? You aren't happy to see me, Malcolm?"

"Eva, why are you doing this? You know this is my home with my wife. You can't be here. Please, I already promised to meet up with you tomorrow. What more do you want?"

"Baby, I just couldn't wait until tomorrow to see you. The more I thought about never having you inside of me again, the more I needed you right now. I mean, she's asleep anyway, isn't she? And don't you miss me already, Malcolm? Aren't you going to miss *all of this?*"

Before I could utter a word, she opened her coat to show her fully naked body in all its glory. I wanted her in the worst way possible, but I was frozen in place from the shock of it all. Then right there at my front door, she unzipped my pants, dropped to her knees, and stuffed all of me inside her mouth. I knew good and damn well that what was happening was completely wrong, but the rush of it all excited me beyond my wildest dreams. Eva had never done anything as insane as that very moment. Yet, part of me loved every single minute of it.

Afraid and highly aroused all at the same time, I tried to pull away, but her mouth gripped tighter. All I could do was hold on to the door and hang on for dear life as my eyes rolled into the back of my head with pure pleasure. Although it took some time for me to let go of whatever I had left inside of me, I finally felt my knees begin to buckle. Instantly, her motion became faster, and her mouth became warmer and wetter when finally, my climax was in sight. It took all that I had not to yell out loud in total and complete euphoria. And as I opened my eyes and tried to steady myself, I watched her wipe her lips, smile, and blow me a kiss as she tied her coat and walked back to her car.

All in a flash, she left just as suddenly as she had come, and I was left standing in my doorway, with my pants to my ankles, and downright stunned. At that very second, I wasn't sure how I would ever let go of Eva—or if she'd let me. Then as I pulled up my slacks, closed the door, and set the alarm, the unthinkable happened.

"Malcolm?" I heard Mariah call out. I swear, if I could have crapped on myself at that very second, I certainly would have. But instead, we met in the kitchen as she walked to the refrigerator with squinted eyes.

"Baby, what are you doing awake?" I asked, hoping she hadn't seen or heard anything.

"My mouth was dry, and I had no water on the nightstand. But what are you doing up? I thought you went to bed right after me."

"Uh, I forgot to set the alarm, and you know how I am about that."

"Yeah, I know. Well, c'mon, let's get some sleep."

I followed right behind her to our bedroom, but after what had just happened, little did she know sleep would be the furthest thing from my mind.

Chapter 7

Crystal

"I think tonight went much better than we expected, don't you?" Cedric asked after coming out of the shower and getting into bed.

"Yeah, sure, it was okay, I guess."

"You guess? What do you mean? You got to see Mariah, she could see CJ for the first time, and thankfully, you didn't kill Malcolm. I would say that was grounds for a perfect night." He laughed as if he'd made the joke of the year, yet there was nothing at all funny in my opinion. I had a much more crucial matter at the forefront of my mind than if the night had gone well.

"Cedric, there's something I need to ask you. I probably should have dealt with this long ago, but I didn't, and I think it's time that I do now. First, however, you must promise me that you will be completely honest with me and that it will remain between only us."

"Wow, whatever it is sounds deep. What's wrong, baby?"

"Promise me first that it will never go beyond these four walls."

"Yeah, of course, sweetheart. You can ask me anything. You already know whatever we talk about is strictly between us. Now, what's going on?"

"Well, it's about the night before Mariah and Malcolm's wedding. Cedric, was he with another woman?"

"Oh, Crystal." He sat up and rubbed his head with both hands before answering. I could tell by the expression on his face that my question caught him off guard, and he wasn't sure how to respond. "What exactly do you mean 'with another woman'?"

"C'mon, Ced, I don't have to spell it out to you. Was Malcolm with another woman that night?"

"Honey, no, not at all. I mean, it was the night before the man's wedding, so did we have women there? Yes, we did. We had several strippers if you need to know the dirty little details. But if you're trying to ask me if my best friend did anything inappropriate with anyone before marrying Mariah, the answer is a firm no. And trust me. I know that for a fact because there's no way I would have let something like that take place. So, besides getting a couple of lap dances and tossing around some dollar bills here and there, Malcolm was on his best behavior."

I glared at him momentarily, searching for truth and honesty behind his eyes. It wasn't like Cedric to lie to me, and I could tell he was being honest.

"And, anyway, baby, why are you asking me about something that happened almost ten years ago with Malcolm?"

"All right, listen, Cedric. I guess I need to come clean. As I said, maybe I should have said something way before tonight. I've tried to put it out of my mind all this time, but I just can't any longer. See, I, um, I came to where you, Malcolm, and the other groomsmen were staying that night. But to tell the truth, I really can't even remember why," I said, outright lying before he quickly interrupted my thoughts.

"Baby, hold on. I don't remember you coming there that night."

"Well, that's just it, Cedric. You don't remember be-cause when I got there, I saw Malcolm . . . and some woman. Honey, I saw him hug and kiss her like they were together. It was weird. And before he saw me, I just got back inside my car and left."

"And you've never said anything about it this entire time?" he stated matter-of-factly.

"No."

"And that is why you've hated Malcolm all these years, and it had nothing to do with him making me late to your birthday party?"

"Right."

He got out of bed and started walking around, making me panic. I wasn't sure if he was about to tell me some deep, dark secret he shared with his best friend or what.

"Baby, so, what are you thinking? Do you know the woman Malcolm was with?"

"Crystal!" He raised his voice. "Please stop saying that and put it out of your head, okay? Malcolm wasn't with another woman. I honestly don't know what or who you saw, but I'm sure whatever it was was harmless. So, please, baby, promise me you won't run to Mariah with some crazy theory of something practically ten years ago."

"Even if I think he may still be cheating on her? Even if she already has suspicions herself? Do you want me to sit back and remain quiet? Is *that* what you're saying? Because I just want to be totally clear here."

"Baby, I want you to do exactly what you've done for all these years and leave well enough alone, all right? It's their marriage, and only they should deal with it."

"Wow, are you serious right now, Cedric? Because if you were having an affair with someone, and my best friend knew about it, I would definitely expect her to tell me. Not just leave it for us to deal with. I mean, because if that's the case, you're just going right along with whatever he's doing."

"First of all, you don't know if the man is doing any-thing. What you *think* you may have seen was ten years ago. And I'm not going along with anything. But as I said, that's not our issue. It's theirs," he pleaded, but I wasn't trying to hear it.

"You know what, Cedric? If that's truly how you feel, then so be it. But I will need you to sleep in the guest room until you see my point of view and not take up for your sorry excuse of a best friend. I don't want you next to me."

"Oh, give me a break, woman. You *can't* be serious."

"I'm dead serious," I yelled, throwing a pillow at him and tossing our top blanket too.

"Okay, I'll go. But I will say this first . . . If you tell Mariah what you believe you saw all those years ago, and she hates you for it, don't say I didn't tell you so." He walked out of our bedroom, slamming the door behind him. I immediately heard CJ start crying from his baby monitor.

Getting up to see about my son, I was so heated from our exchange that one could probably see smoke coming from my ears. I hated that Cedric was so passive and clueless about things, especially concerning Malcolm. It was like he would take up for the man even if it meant going against me—his own wife. That was the very truth behind Malcolm's words earlier in the kitchen. I was in love with him in high school and not Cedric. My husband simply wasn't the strong, confident, popular young man that Malcolm was in school and certainly not the successful, powerful, and financially stable man that Malcolm was now. I remembered flirting with Malcolm and throwing myself at him throughout high school, but he never took the bait. Instead, his best friend, Cedric Simmons, had approached me, and I settled for him. After all these years, I grew to love my husband despite my hidden feelings for his best friend.

And true enough, deep down, I knew he was likely correct. If I pushed this too far with Mariah, she could very well end up hating me. That was the very reason I had to wait until I had some concrete evidence of who this Eva woman was and Malcolm's extracurricular activities. Then and only then would everyone come to know how serious I was . . . especially Mariah.

Chapter 8

Malcolm

My eyes popped open, and from the looks of the clock's display, I'd only slept about a good hour or so. It had taken me forever to doze off. After thinking about Eva's late-night shenanigans, Crystal's nosiness and accusations, and simply trying to keep Mariah at bay, my mind was much too tangled for any ounce of sleep. However, I suppose that fatigue got the best of me, and I was out without realizing it. Now that I was awake, though, my main objective for the day was settling this matter with Eva. Although my nature started to rise at the mere thought of what had happened, I needed to get focused and ensure she knew it couldn't occur again.

However, after picking up my cell phone, it seemed I spoke too quickly. All I saw were nude pictures of her in that same damn trench coat and heels over my screen.

"Dammit, Eva. Why won't you stop this madness?"

"Who are you talking to in here, sleepyhead?" Mariah said, coming in already dressed and fully made up for the day. She walked over and kissed my lips while I fumbled around, trying to slide my cell phone under the pillow.

"Huh? What? I was, uh, talking to myself about everything I need to take care of today."

"Really? Well, I was hoping I didn't wake you while I dressed. You were sleeping so peacefully. I was beginning to think you would sleep the whole morning away."

"Yeah, I guess I must have been way more exhausted than I thought. But on another note, you are looking beautifully radiant this morning. Should I be nervous? Does someone have a breakfast date that I need to know about?" I joked with her but with a slight seriousness behind my words. My wife was extremely attractive, and just like Eva, she could have any man she wanted. And although I hadn't shown it through my actions over the years, I planned on showing her every chance I could how honored I was that she chose me.

"No, honey, no date at all, but I should have a bit of a surprise for you when I return," she answered with her face lit up.

"Surprise? Baby, now, you know I really don't like surprises."

"I know, but I have a feeling you're going to love this, especially if it all plays out the way I hope. In fact, I *know* you're going to love it."

"All right, now my curiosity is getting the best of me. What is it?"

"Honey, you'll need to wait until I get back, and maybe then I'll tell you everything, but for right now, my lips are sealed. Anyway, what are your plans for the day?"

"Um, I have a business meeting this afternoon."

"A business meeting? On a Saturday? You haven't done that in a long time."

"I know, but today was the only time my client could meet. It shouldn't take long at all, though."

"Oh, then where will you be? I can come by after my appointment and have a lunch date. And then maybe I can share my surprise with you," she said, and I realized I'd put my foot in my mouth and said too much.

"Baby, why don't we make that a dinner date instead? I don't think the meeting will last long, but I never know."

"Oh, okay. Well, I will see you back here at the house later then."

"Sounds good."

She kissed me again and left. I couldn't have been more relieved because, just like I figured, Eva had started repeatedly texting me. I could clearly see she wasn't about to allow me to call it quits without giving me a run for my money. With that said, I knew I had to come up with something to make her back down for good. I had no clue what that was because, from the looks of it, she was holding the cards *and* my balls in the palm of her hand.

Chapter 9

Mariah

As I got inside my truck to head to my destination, I was outdone with the overall sense of peace regarding my marriage compared to just a few hours ago. After the way he'd made love to me, I knew any thoughts of Malcolm cheating had been all in my head. My husband loved me, regardless of what anyone else thought, including Crystal. And now I was headed to take the first step in showing him just how much I loved him too. I would give my husband the one thing I knew his heart desired all these years, and I wanted to do it for our tenth anniversary. Seeing that look in his eyes last night as he held CJ and played with him and loved on him confirmed what I knew deep down inside. My husband wanted a son, and I would do everything possible to give him one. True enough, we'd been trying for so long that I'd almost lost hope. I almost believed that maybe children weren't in the cards for us. But holding CJ last night did something to me. It ignited a flame that I thought fizzled out long ago. Having him in my arms told me what I needed to get my mind and heart focused again, and I knew it would make Malcolm the happiest man alive.

I turned the music up and began singing along to one of Beyoncé's latest tracks while cruising through the morning traffic. At least, that was until I saw Crystal's name flashing across the screen on my front dashboard as I was trying to hit a couple of high notes. Part of me wondered whether I needed to answer. I knew she would have a million questions about where I was headed so early on Saturday, but I wasn't quite ready to share that information with her. Frankly, I didn't need any negativity before my appointment. Plus, if and when it did happen, I wanted it to remain between Malcolm and me before we shared the news with anyone else. Sure, it may have seemed a little superstitious, but I didn't care. I couldn't afford to let anything jinx the outcome. However, despite my better judgment, I decided to answer anyway.

"Hello?"

"Hey, girl. Well, it sounds like you're up and out rather early this morning."

"Yeah, and it sounds like you just barely rolled over. Are you all right? Did you have a tough night with my little CJ?"

"More like a tough night with Big Cedric, honestly. We had somewhat of an argument last night."

"Oh no, I hope everything is all right. Do you want to talk about it?"

"Not really. Not right now, anyway. Maybe later, if it turns into one of those things we'll end up laughing about in the end. But enough about me and my problems. What do you have going on today? I was hoping to stop by and see you after my appointment this afternoon."

"Sure. What time were you thinking?"

"Depending on my appointment, I'm thinking around three."

"Yeah, that should be perfect. My appointment should be over way before then."

"Okay, and do you know if Malcolm will be home?"

"Malcolm? Um, I'm not sure. He has a business meeting this afternoon around that time, so probably not."

"Perfect. Well, I'll see you then, okay?" She sounded better than when she first called once I said Malcolm wouldn't be home.

"Hey, before you go, you're bringing the baby, right?"

"Uh, no, not this time. He's going to have some father-son time with his daddy."

"Bummer. Well, okay, I guess you'll just have to do."

We both burst out laughing at my last comment before hanging up. I loved my best friend dearly, but I must admit that her behavior had been a bit off the past couple of days. I wasn't sure if it was because we hadn't seen each other in a while or possibly even postpartum blues. Either way, it was beginning to concern me, especially when she asked about Malcolm and her mood changed drastically when she found out he wouldn't be there. For both of them to say that they had settled their differences last night, they were still acting pretty strange when it came to each other. However, after pulling up to the doctor's office, I put their issues on the back burner. I had a much more important issue to be concerned about.

Walking in, a sense of excitement hit me. All kinds of what-ifs started to circulate through my mind. What if the doctor told me I was already pregnant? Although I hadn't felt any different than usual, my cycle was about three days late, which gave me a little glimpse of hope. Then again, what if she said I wasn't? I couldn't help but wonder how long it would take for us to get pregnant. Being overwhelmed was an understatement, but the adrenaline from the unknown outweighed it all.

Walking up to the receptionist, I gave her my name, and after all the standard preliminaries, I was in a room wearing a paper gown with my legs dangling from the bed shortly after. Someone knocked on the door a second later, and Dr. Taylor walked in.

"Well, hello there, Mariah. How are you doing today?"

"I'm doing good, Dr. Taylor, but I hope to be a lot better by the time I leave here if I get the news I'm expecting," I said. Although I would have expected a little enthusiasm from her from my response, she appeared the total opposite. Surprisingly, it took her a moment before she began to speak again.

"Mariah, I've been your doctor for quite some time now, and I pride myself on being your doctor and your friend."

"I'm sorry, Dr. Taylor, but why are you telling me this? Is something wrong?"

"Well, I know how much you want to have a baby. . . ." Her words faded off toward the end.

"So, basically, you're saying I'm not pregnant, right? That's okay," I said after preparing myself for the news. "That only means Malcolm and I must continue trying."

"Well . . ." She looked down at her clipboard instead of directly at me. "It's a bit more than that," she said, which suddenly had me confused and in a panic.

"What do you mean?"

"Mariah, there's no easy way to say this other than to come out and tell you. You have fibroids, and I suggest you have a full hysterectomy."

"A hysterectomy? But-but, then that would mean that—"

"You won't ever be able to have children." She finished my sentence after seeing the tears beginning to drip from my eyes.

"Wow, I wasn't quite expecting this news. I'm so sorry for crying right now." I wiped my eyes, and she grabbed some tissue from a table in the corner and handed it to me.

"Now you know you don't have to apologize. I know how much you wanted a child with your husband."

"Um, so is that my only option? A hysterectomy and that's it? I mean, should I have a second opinion?"

"Of course, you can always get another opinion. I would never steer my patients away from that, but honestly, any other gynecologist will likely tell you the same thing. We could try different things like a laser to remove the fibroids or even a partial hysterectomy. However, having those alternative types of surgery will still put your fertility at risk. If you were able to get pregnant, it might be complicated to carry a child full term."

"So, in other words, you're saying that either way, I'm screwed, and a child is just not in Malcolm's and my future."

The room became quiet and colder than it already was. I got the feeling she didn't quite know what to say, and I was already trying to figure out a way to break the news to Malcolm. At least, that was until she went in a different direction that caught me totally off guard.

"Mariah, can I take off my doctor's hat for a moment and put on my friend's hat?"

"Sure."

"I probably have no business going here, but do you believe in God?"

"Uh, I, uh, I, yes, I do. I mean, I'm not in church every week, and I don't carry my Bible around with me, and I probably don't pray as much as I should, but I still believe in Him. But why would you ask me something like that?"

"I asked because of two things. One is I believe that everything happens for a reason. You might need to get the hysterectomy, but a child may come into your life in another way, shape, or form."

"You mean like adoption or surrogacy?"

"Yes. There are many children out here without parents to love or care for them the way I know you and Malcolm would. Or, as you said, surrogacy is also a real option."

"No, I'm sorry, but that's just not for me, Dr. Taylor. Call me silly, but I think I've watched too many Lifetime movies where the woman turns out to be crazy and wants your child *and* your husband."

"Okay. Or you could have the fibroids lasered, get pregnant, carry the child to term, and have a fully healthy baby. It could be a long shot, but it's also very much possible."

"But I'm confused. Which one are you suggesting?"

"Listen, the doctor side of me has to tell you that a full hysterectomy would be the best option. I've looked at your X-rays, and you have many of them, some golf ball-size and some bigger. Yet, the friend, human, and Christian sides of me are saying simply to trust God for a miracle. But still and all, the end decision is totally up to you. However, whatever you choose to do, we need to do it as soon as possible, and I would need to prepare you for whatever risks might come with them."

"I see."

"Look, Mariah, I don't need an answer today or even tomorrow. So please, take some time with Malcolm, and you two sit down and figure out what you believe would be best. And more importantly, pray to God to direct you in what you should do. I believe he'll give you the right choice."

"Okay, Dr. Taylor, but please, can you do me a favor?"

"Of course, anything."

"Malcolm can't know about this until I'm ready. So I don't want him to know I came here today or about anything you just talked to me about, please."

"Honey, are you sure about that? I mean, of course, I have to respect your privacy as my patient, but I do feel that you should discuss this with your husband. You shouldn't make any decisions about this alone."

"Trust me, I hear you, Dr. Taylor, but my decision stands. Whatever I decide, my husband can never know."

"Okay. I just hope you know what you're doing, Mariah."

"I do. I'm saving my marriage. That's what I'm doing."

Thankfully, I made it to my truck without passing out. I had started to perspire, and my stomach felt like a million butterflies were fluttering inside of it. Then my mouth got dry, and I had the strangest taste. Then before I knew it, I turned my head and puked all over the ground. The entire time, tears still hadn't stopped flowing from my eyes.

I kept trying to pull myself together, but that was much easier said than done. All I knew was I needed to leave that parking lot as quickly as possible. My goal was to get home and figure out one of two things. Either I would break down and tell Malcolm that we would never have a child together, or I had to think of a way to give this man the son I knew he desired. My mind and heart were leaning toward the latter, despite how deceitful it might have seemed.

Chapter 10

Malcolm

It was two o'clock on the dot. I'd been waiting at a corner table in the back of the coffee shop for at least ten minutes. I would have figured that after all the stunts Eva pulled, acting as if it was so urgent to see me, she would have arrived by now. Yet, I should have known better. In true Eva fashion, she had to make an entrance and did just that as she strolled in. She wore a black, skintight dress with black open-toed heels to match. The dress gripped her in all the right places and appeared as if it were painted on. I watched her pull off her shades and fling her long, curly hair while looking around until her eyes caught mine. A slight smirk came across her face before she swished her fine ass in my direction.

I could only imagine what she had worked out in her mind to try to change my mind about things. But regardless of what she said, I planned on sticking to my guns with my decision. However, just like last night, I was afraid she'd make it extremely hard to do that. Her sex appeal was on a thousand today, and truth be told, I wanted her in the worst way. It was taking everything inside of me not to hop up, take her to our normal meeting spot, and have my way with her.

"Well, hello, there, Mr. Carter."

"Hey, Eva," I tried to say casually to make it seem like her beauty didn't entice me.

"Oh, so, no hug and you're not going to pull out my chair?" she questioned while still standing and looking at me as if I'd better get up.

I stood up and wrapped my arms around her tiny waist as she put her arms around my neck. Her scent was sweet and delicious. I'd bought it over the years, and she wore it every time we were together. Her skin held it well, and I almost didn't want to think of never smelling it again. Quickly coming back to my senses, I let go of her embrace and pulled out her chair.

"Eva, you know this isn't a date or anything, and I can't be here too long with you. I don't need anyone to see us in public like this."

"So, is that why you wanted to meet on this side of town? It took me some time to get here."

"Well, I'm a married man," I reminded her. "Being out with a woman like you already draws much attention. If someone I knew saw me, there would be a million questions or accusations all around town."

"I see." I could tell she wasn't thrilled with my response.

"So, what's up? Why did you want to meet?"

She took a sip of water sitting on the table, and looked at me like she couldn't care less about everything I'd said before that moment.

"Malcolm, you know exactly why we're here. It's about us."

"Uh, wait. Stop, Eva." I tried not to raise my voice and even lowered my talking to a whisper. "There is no 'us,' okay? Like I said yesterday, I hate ending things the way I did, but it's honestly for the best. I hope you can understand that and get past all of this. And just so I make myself very clear, things like coming to my home or sending me nude photos first thing in the morning can never, ever happen again."

She cracked the same little smirk across her face as if I'd told a joke or something.

"All right, so here's the thing, Malcolm. You're acting as if you hold all the cards in your hand. However, both of us know that I do. Now, I came to your home and sent those pictures to show you how easy it would be to destroy your whole world if I wanted to."

"And is that *really* what you want, though? To destroy my whole world?"

She took a second or two to answer as if she were actually contemplating it.

"No, it's not what I want, but I promise I *will* do it if I don't have any other choice."

"Wow, are you *really* doing this with me, of all people? Eva, you're far from that quiet and shy young lady I knew all those years ago. But then again, maybe I created this devil in a black dress sitting before me, huh?" I said. Then, before she could say anything more, my eyes caught a glimpse of the one person I would never have expected to be there. "Oh, shit," I let slip out.

"What? What's wrong with you? You look like you've seen a ghost or something."

"Don't turn around now, but my wife's best friend just came in. It looks like she's ordering something, but she's the last person I need to see us together." I was nervous. "She was the one I mentioned I needed to talk to you about on the phone yesterday. She let it slip that she saw us that night before my wedding all those years ago. She saw me kiss you."

"Really? And she's just *now* saying something about it?"

"That's what I questioned too. She claimed she didn't want to hurt Mariah."

"So, did she overhear you talking to me or something on the phone last night?"

"Uh, no. Well, at least I don't think so. Why would you ask that?"

"Malcolm, don't you find it a little too coincidental that she showed up at this particular Starbucks right around this time while we're here?"

"Yeah, you're right. That does seem a little strange. Especially when there are several stores closer to her home."

"Well, if she heard you on the phone with me, she's either spying for your wife or simply just being nosy."

"Either way, I don't want to take any chances. We may have to finish this conversation later, especially since she just looked this way," I said with Crystal's eyes staring right into mine from the to-go counter. I knew I needed to get a handle on things quickly because I was in the midst of two women who could totally destroy me, and I had no idea what to do for the first time in forever.

"Listen, if she didn't say anything about the night before your wedding, then she will most likely not say anything now. So, please, get a grip. Besides, Malcolm, I need to tell you something before we leave here today. It's the real reason I wanted to meet. It's something I think I should have told you as soon as I found out. In fact, I know I should have."

"And what's that?" I asked, keeping my eyes on Crystal as I watched her find a table across the room. My mind was no longer on Eva as I thought about what Crystal had said in her kitchen yesterday about seeing me the day before my wedding. Suddenly, my gut told me that Eva was right. She had to know I would be here, but I couldn't figure out how for the life of me, since I was closed up in Cedric's media room. And the other thing that Eva was right about was that if she were going to tell Mariah anything, she would have done it already. So, instead, I believed she showed up here strictly to taunt me.

"Malcolm? Malcolm?" Eva had been calling me without me realizing it. "What I need to tell you about is this," she said, pushing what looked like a digital photo before me.

"What in the world is this?" I asked, wondering why on earth she would bring me all the way here for something like this. "I mean, you're not about to try to pull some craziness just to keep me around, are you?"

"Malcolm, please, just listen to me because I don't have an easy way to say this."

"Say what? Whatever it is, you may as well go ahead and spill it already, but like I said yesterday, Eva, it won't change my decision."

I watched her drink more water and take a deep breath before speaking. "All right, here goes. Malcolm, I'm-I'm-I'm—"

"Spit it out already. You're what?"

"I'm pregnant, Malcolm. I'm pregnant with *your* baby and won't abort it this time as I did before."

Chapter 11

Eva

"You're pregnant? Really? Is this some type of joke you're trying to play on me, Eva? Some ploy just for me to stay in your life?" he asked.

"It's not a joke, Malcolm, and it's not something I would say just to keep you around. As I said, I should have told you when I first found out, but I just couldn't—"

"So, if it's true, then why tell me now?" He cut me off. "If you couldn't bring yourself to do it when you first knew about it, then why do it now? I mean, did you think I was just going to say okay and leave my wife, and then me, you, and this so-called baby would run off and live happily ever after? Is *that* what you thought?"

"Listen, Malcolm, I don't quite know what I thought, but I knew I needed to tell you before you walked completely out of this baby's life."

"And yours too, right? You meant before I walk out of *your* life, right, Eva? You know, you are a real piece of work," he said. "So, if you're pregnant, why can't I tell? I mean, your clothing is so skintight, I'm surprised that you can even breathe. Not to mention the fact that I've seen you naked. Remember last night? You sure didn't look pregnant then. And then what is all this business about not having an abortion like before? *When* before, Eva?"

"Look, I never said anything, but I was pregnant after our first time together right before you left for college. And maybe you don't remember sleeping with me because I was considered so awkward and ugly back then. Or maybe our relationship didn't count because you were so ashamed that you couldn't tell your family or friends about me. But it happened, and I came up pregnant."

"Listen, I never said I was ashamed of you back then, Eva. You have to know that, and it was just the situation I was in. I was young and dumb and didn't know how to handle things. But if anything, I was the one that took up for you, if you don't remember. *I* was the one that protected you and the one that loved you when no one else did."

"I do remember that," I said, with his words meaning so much to me. "And, Malcolm, I've always appreciated that about you."

"But you didn't appreciate me enough to be honest with me back then or even now?"

"Listen, it happened, and you left, and we never spoke about it afterward. I didn't know I was pregnant until you were already gone. And I wanted to call and tell you, but I also didn't want to ruin your life back then, Malcolm. So, I thought I was doing what was right by not saying anything and not having the baby, but—"

"But you don't mind ruining my life now?"

"Look, I get that you're upset. I do, but that doesn't change the fact that I am carrying *your* child, and in a few months, it will be here with us."

He got quiet and looked as if he were thinking. I hated springing this on him, especially right in the middle of Starbucks, but I felt he gave me no other choice. Of course, I wanted him to stay in my life, but more than that, I needed him to remain in our child's life.

"Malcolm, don't you have anything to say?"

"What do you want me to say? You tell me after all these years that we had a child together . . . but that you had an abortion . . . and now you're pregnant again, and you ask if I have anything to say? How am I supposed to take all of this in right now? How do I tell my wife about this, Eva?"

"I don't know, Malcolm. I don't have the answer for that," I said.

"Yeah, well, I don't either. I gotta go."

"Wait, wait a minute." I grabbed his arm as he stood up. "Now what? Where do we go from here?"

"I'll figure this out, and you'll hear from me soon."

He left without saying another word to me, and I wasn't sure how I felt then. I didn't know if I felt more relieved that he had finally learned the truth or more hurt by his nonresponse to it all. The only thing I did know was that I still wouldn't back down. No matter what Malcolm decided, in the end, either he would make sure this baby and I were well off—or I would. And if it were left up to me, I would take every dime he and that wife of his had. Now, all I wanted to do was get home and love on my unborn child . . . at least that was until I saw her walking in my direction.

"Excuse me, miss," she said, standing there with the dumbest look on her face.

"Yes?"

"I'm sorry to bother you, but was that Malcolm Carter that just left? I'm only asking because he and I went to high school together, and I haven't seen him in ages, but I know that was him. He honestly hasn't changed a bit."

"Uh, yes, that was Malcolm Carter. He's . . . my attorney. And what was your name so I can tell him I ran into you?"

"Oh, I'm Terri. And you are?"

"I didn't say," I said, grabbing my bag, standing up, and walking right out the door, leaving her there. However, little did she know I wasn't done with her. She was too damn nosy for her own good, and I would make sure she kept her mouth closed when it came to Malcolm and me.

Chapter 12

Crystal

Before making myself comfortable at a table, I looked Malcolm directly in the eyes. I wanted him to see me there because when I planned to say something to my friend, he wouldn't be able to weasel his way out and say it wasn't him.

I made it there a little after two, and after ordering my favorite drink, I scoped the room, hoping to see him. Just my luck, my eyes caught hold of him and the woman sitting far off in a back corner. She was incredibly sexy and attractive from head to toe. Simply looking at her made me feel somewhat sorry for my best friend. I mean, it wasn't that Mariah wasn't beautiful in her own way, but there was something magnetic about this woman that no one could deny. I could see why Malcolm, or any man, for that matter, would be drawn to her.

A few minutes after sitting down to get an eyeful of them together, I noticed how it almost looked as if they were in some heated exchange. Malcolm seemed angry, while she seemed sorry or apologetic. Whatever it was, though, must have had him furious because, out of nowhere, I watched him get up and abruptly leave. I hoped he wasn't running out because of me, but it wasn't like I cared anyway.

However, with him gone, I figured it was my chance to go over and meet the woman. But after introducing myself and trying to play nice, she came off pretty rude and brash and left just as quickly and abruptly as Malcolm had.

What the hell is going on with you two, Malcolm? Who is this woman, and what exactly are your dealings with her? I asked myself. I immediately knew I had to do some digging to learn more about her. That whole theory of Malcolm being her attorney and her being a client was nothing more than some big fat lie. She didn't come off believable at all, and a blind man could see straight through her words. Then there was the scent she'd left behind as she walked past me. It had to be what Mariah was referring to yesterday. So, with that in mind, I knew her name was Eva and that she'd possibly been involved with Malcolm for at least a couple of months. Outside of that, I didn't have much to go on, but my gut told me she had to be the same woman I had seen him kissing the night before his wedding. My memory hadn't always been the best, so as that night replayed, I tried to recall her features or anything that would connect her to this woman. Yet, I continued to draw a blank. But my woman's intuition never steered me wrong. It had to be her. I just *knew* it.

"Wow, you've been cheating on my friend your entire marriage. You sorry, good-for-nothing bastard."

I hurried to pay my bill and headed out to my car. Although I hadn't put everything together, I was still going to put a little bug in Mariah's ear that her suspicions regarding her husband were correct. I knew that Cedric told me not to get involved, but after seeing this woman and her exchange with Malcolm, I had no other choice. I had to.

Once I walked across the street and opened the door to my car, that crazy broad jumped out of her car, walked up to mine, and slammed my door shut.

"What the hell are you doing?" I yelled.

"Making sure you know exactly where I stand, Crystal," she said, confirming that Malcolm had told her about me. So, with that, I decided to play her game right along with her.

"You'll get out of my way if you know what's good for you, Eva. You don't want to play these games with me."

"See, that's where you are wrong, my dear. I have nothing at all to lose. You, on the other hand, have everything to lose. So, I'm going to say this to you once and one time only. Stay the fuck out of Malcolm's and my business, or I will make you, your husband, and that sweet little newborn baby of yours *my* business. Got it?"

She returned to her car, got in, and sped off, leaving me standing there. I tried my hardest to play the tough-girl role, but I became afraid the second she mentioned CJ. I even thought I felt a drop of urine trickle down my leg. My hand shook as I tried to open the car door.

"Breathe, Crystal, just breathe," I told myself once I finally got inside. As tears slowly started to creep down my face, I began to think about what my next move should be. Although I wanted to be there for my best friend, something told me I needed to take this woman at her word. I couldn't afford to allow any harm to come to me, Cedric, or, more importantly, CJ because of Malcolm's behavior.

Chapter 13

Mariah

Luckily, Malcolm hadn't made it home yet. Even though I dreaded telling him the truth, I decided on the drive home that was what I needed to do. He and I had never lied or kept things from each other, and I didn't want to start now—especially with something like this.

I took the scenic route home to give myself time to think about everything Dr. Taylor said, and I decided she was absolutely right. There were other options, and I planned on giving my husband a child one way or another. In fact, our tenth anniversary was a few months away, and I was determined to make that his anniversary gift. I decided that I wasn't going to settle on one option either. I would try anything and everything until one of them worked.

Walking into the kitchen, I threw my cell phone and purse on the island and went to the refrigerator to get bottled water. But before I could do that, someone rang the bell repeatedly like the police were behind them. I went to the door as quickly as possible and found Crystal standing there, breathing heavily and looking in a panic.

"Hey, girl. Are you all right? The way you were ringing, I would have thought someone was after you."

"No, I'm fine. I just drank a lot of water on the way and needed to release myself. But is Malcolm home?"

"Uh, no, he hasn't made it here yet, but what does he have to do with you going to the bathroom?"

"I'll talk to you when I come out."

She went inside the half bathroom near the front door while I returned to the kitchen to pour us some drinks. Although it was still early afternoon, I felt we could use an excellent smooth wine to settle us down. Me, because of the news I had received from the doctor, and Crystal because of her disagreement with Cedric. I never really knew them to argue about much throughout the years, so it was shocking to hear. However, whatever it was, I was optimistic they would get past it soon enough. A second later, she walked into the kitchen, much more relieved than when she had arrived.

"Girl, you must have had a gallon of water or something," I joked around with her, trying to remove the stern look on her face.

"Only a couple of glasses, but you know how I am about public bathrooms, so I held it until I got here, which was a huge mistake. Anyway, Malcolm didn't come in, did he?"

"Crystal, no, honey, Malcolm is not home. But what is wrong with you? Why are you so worried about Malcolm's whereabouts?"

"Um, I'm not worried about him. I mean, I guess I just wanted to make sure that we were good after last night."

"Oh, okay. Well, he and I talked a little last night, and I'm sure that things should be all right between you two from here on out," I said, handing a glass of wine to her and taking a seat at the island.

"Thank you. I really needed this."

"Yeah, I could tell. You weren't quite looking like yourself at the door. Are you sure everything's okay and it's not something more than you drinking a ton of water?" I asked after noticing how she almost appeared to have been crying too.

"Mariah, as I said earlier, it's just my issues with Cedric and being overwhelmed with the newness of having a new baby. It's a lot, and I guess it all just hit me in the car on the way over, that's all."

"I understand. Of course, I can't relate to having a new baby, but I can imagine. And whatever the issue is with Cedric, I'm sure you two will get past it sooner than later. You and Cedric have been together all these years, and I've never seen two people more made for each other. In fact, to be honest, I've always envied what you all share. I mean, although what Malcolm and I share is good, it's not like you and Cedric. Love exudes from you guys. It's practically unreal."

"Girl, I appreciate that, but Cedric and I have our ups and downs and trials just like the next couple. Trust me. It's nothing to envy."

"I hear you, but now you all have CJ, and your family is complete. So, if I can offer any advice, go home and do what you must do to make up with your man. I'm sure whatever the disagreement was, it was something trivial and not worth losing sleep over."

"Thanks, I appreciate that. I really do. But, Mariah, if I can change the subject a bit, I need to tell you something."

"What is it? Whatever it is sounds serious."

"It is, and I probably should have said something a long time ago, but—"

"Hey, ladies." Malcolm walked in right in the middle of Crystal's sentence. "I hope I'm not interrupting anything."

"No, honey, you're not. We're just having a glass of wine and some girl time. But how was your business meeting today?"

"It was good, baby," he said, giving me a big smooch on the lips before taking bottled water out of the refrigerator. I didn't want to think it, believe it, or admit it, but the second he leaned in, I could smell that same fragrance again. "Well, please don't let me intrude on you all's girl time. Just act like I'm not even here, all right?" He moved around the kitchen, grabbing things to make a sandwich. On the other hand, I tried to get back to whatever it was Crystal was trying to tell me until she had a sudden change of plans.

"Um, actually, I'm going to head home and relieve Cedric of his daddy duties. He's been with CJ all morning and afternoon, and I'm sure the baby is probably grumpy by now and wants his mommy."

"Wait, I thought you had something that you needed to tell me?"

"Uh, why don't we try to link up tomorrow sometime and talk then?"

"Are you sure?"

"I'm positive." She immediately grabbed her bag and headed toward the door.

"Okay, then maybe you and the baby can stop by after you leave church. I mean, if it's not too soon to take him out?"

"Wow, don't you sound like someone's mother all of a sudden?" she said, and little did she know, it struck a nerve with me. Suddenly, I was reminded I would never sound like someone's mother.

Trying my best not to think about what had happened at the doctor's office, I waited until we'd gotten outside and returned to whatever she needed to tell me before Malcolm walked in. I grabbed her arm before she went to her car.

"Hey, are you *sure* you're all right? I mean, it almost feels like your sudden need to leave has something to do with Malcolm. This isn't about last night again, is it?"

"Mariah, nothing's wrong, and my leaving has nothing to do with your husband. I just need to get home to my own husband and son. They need me."

"Okay, well, I'll call you tomorrow when I think you're out of church. I love you, Crystal." I hugged her and watched her get inside her car. So much of me wanted to believe in what she was saying. However, I probably knew my best friend better than she knew herself. She could say a million times that her odd behavior and urgency to leave had nothing to do with Malcolm, but something told me otherwise. I needed to get to the bottom of what was really going on between them, and if she wouldn't tell me, then he would.

I returned to the kitchen, where Malcolm had finished a sandwich and beer. The second he saw me, he pulled me close and put his arms around my waist, kissing me on the cheek.

"Sweetie, are you good? You seem like something's bothering you."

"I'm okay, Malcolm," was all I managed to get out while trying to think of what to address first—whether it was Crystal's strange behavior or what had happened at the doctor's office.

"Are you sure, baby? I mean, I haven't seen you all day, and this is all the love I get?"

"I'm sorry, honey. I've just had a long day so far. Plus, there are some things that I need to talk to you about," I said, wanting desperately to forget about the scent on his clothing and tell him the other news as quickly as possible.

"Baby, do you think it can wait until later?" he asked, going to the sink and putting his plate and glass in it. "After my day, I'm just a little mentally drained and not up for some deep discussion. Especially not one that might involve your best friend."

"Well, I'm sorry, but it really can't wait. I need to talk to you now."

"All right, all right, sweetie," he said in a much more concerned manner, pulling me into his arms. "What's wrong?"

"I didn't tell you this morning, but I went to see Dr. Taylor."

"Your gynecologist? Why? Was something wrong?"

"No, nothing was wrong before I left, but this morning, I thought Dr. Taylor would tell me I was pregnant or at least help me get pregnant. I thought we would be celebrating right now."

"See, I knew this would happen," he said, pulling away from me.

"You knew what would happen?"

"This whole baby business. We went to see CJ last night, and now Angie believes she's pregnant, and you want a baby too. I mean, haven't we been over this already? Why are you torturing yourself like this? When it happens, it happens. That's it. I'm not hung up on when we have children."

"But that's just it, Malcolm. We will never have children, ever. I have fibroids, and the doctor is recommending a full hysterectomy."

I watched him put both his hands on top of his head. "What? Are you serious? But-but what about a second opinion or something?"

"Sure, she said I was welcome to get a second opinion, but that any gynecologist would say the same thing."

"Okay, okay." He started pacing around. "It's still all right, baby. It's going to be okay. We can always adopt when we're ready or something else. But right now, my only concern is your health and ensuring you are good, okay?" He pulled me back into his arms and held me tight.

I nodded in agreement with what he said, but deep down, I knew that my husband wanted a child, a son, to be exact. I needed to give him that, or I feared losing my marriage altogether—especially if the mystery woman behind the fragrance meant anything to him and could one day give him what I couldn't.

"Malcolm, can I ask you something?"

"Of course, baby. What's up?"

"Do you believe in miracles or the power of prayer? Like, if you were told something would never be possible, do you believe that it could still be possible in the end, through prayer and faith?"

"I-I-I don't know. Why are you asking me this?" he questioned. I knew deep down that he wouldn't exactly know how to respond. Neither my husband nor I had ever been the overly religious type of couple.

"I'm just curious, that's all." I laid my head on his chest as he rubbed my back.

"Listen, we're going to get through this one way or another, whether through technology, medically, or even spiritually. One way or another, we'll get through this. I promise."

Chapter 14

Crystal

After leaving Mariah's, I drove home and sat in the car for a few minutes before going inside. I needed a moment to go over everything that had happened during the day. Not only did I have to worry about this woman Eva, but I was also sure from the look Malcolm had given me in the kitchen that he'd be a huge problem for me too. He knew I was about to tell Mariah about today, as well as what I'd seen that night before their wedding, and if looks could kill, I would have been dead already.

On top of that, I couldn't get past the desire I had the minute I saw him kiss her. I hated the way I felt, but part of me wished it were me that he was kissing. My mind quickly returned to yesterday in the kitchen when I felt his hand inside my panties. Thinking about it at that moment made me long to feel him inside me.

"Stop it, Crystal, stop it. This is your best friend's husband . . . and your husband's best friend. You have to stop wanting this man."

Trying to talk myself out of my feelings and gather my composure, I entered the house and found Cedric on the couch with CJ across his chest. I looked in his direction but didn't say anything, simply trying to gauge the temperature in the room. He must not have been upset anymore because he spoke in his normal Cedric-like manner the minute he saw me. Immediately, that's when I realized why I loved my husband so much. True enough, he wasn't Malcolm, but I never had to guess whether he loved me, and he was all the man I needed.

"Hey, baby."

"Hey, Cedric," I said, kissing him on the lips and picking CJ up off his chest. "It feels so good to be back home and loving on my two favorite men."

"Wow, someone is in a much better mood than last night. So, I take it you had a good day?"

"It was okay," I said, sitting on the couch across from him. "I didn't do much but run a few errands and then sat at Starbucks for a little while, enjoying some me time. Then I ran by Mariah and Malcolm's, but I didn't stay long because I was dying to get home to you for some reason," I said, smiling and hoping he wouldn't sense my false sincerity.

"Good, well, I'm glad you could have some time just to do whatever you wanted, and, baby, I'm sorry about last night. I understand how much Mariah means to you, and I get that you want to be there for her. But I was only saying that sometimes, we can do more harm than good when trying to be there for the people we love, especially concerning matters of the heart."

"You're right, Cedric, and after having time alone to think, I decided to take your advice and not get involved."

"Really? Well, I can't say that I'm not happy about that. I mean, baby, no matter what you believe took place all those years ago, and even if you still don't like Malcolm now, he loves Mariah. They love each other, and unless you have concrete proof that he's been stepping out on her, then please, don't rock the boat. Their tenth anniversary is coming up in a few months, and we both know how difficult it is for a couple to last ten years. So let's help them celebrate that instead of worrying about something that might have happened the night before they married. Life is short, and tomorrow isn't promised to us, so let's enjoy today and leave the past in the past."

I could appreciate all that my husband said, but the second he mentioned having concrete proof, my mind returned to Eva and trying to find out as much about her as possible.

"You're right, baby, and I apologize too. But something interesting did happen today while I was out."

"Really? What's that?"

"I ran into a woman named Eva," I said, trying to see his reaction to see if Malcolm had possibly mentioned her to him. Cedric was never one to have a poker face, so I knew if Malcolm had said anything to him about this woman, he wouldn't be able to fake it. "She said I looked familiar, but I didn't recognize her. It's been bothering me ever since where I might know her from."

"Eva, huh?" He sat up. "You don't find many women named Eva these days, especially around here. I wonder if it's the same person we went to high school with."

"Wait a minute. We went to high school with someone named Eva?" I honestly had no clue, and my ears suddenly stood at attention to everything my husband said.

"Yeah, we did. You probably don't remember because she was pretty quiet and weird, and you hung out more with the popular crowd."

"Weird? In what way?" I inquired.

"Baby, I don't know how to explain it. She was just weird. She always had her head in a book, was extremely quiet and didn't speak to at all, and always sat alone in the lunchroom. If you didn't have any classes with the girl, you wouldn't have even known she was a student there."

I listened to his words and tried to imagine Malcolm with someone like Cedric described. There was no way that was even possible with the type of person Malcolm was in school. He wouldn't have been caught dead with a girl like that. Besides, the woman I saw today wouldn't have been that type of girl in any way, shape, or form. No matter how long ago that was, people don't drastically change like that.

"So, baby, do you remember Malcolm being friends with her?"

"Uh, I don't know," he said, getting up and heading toward the kitchen. "Malcolm was the most popular young man in high school, so I guess it could have been possible. He might have had some classes with her, but I'm sure they weren't best friends. So why are you concerned about Eva and Malcolm anyway, Crystal? And, please, don't lie to me."

"Honey, I was only asking. As I said, I ran into her today, and she was adamant that we knew each other. And now you're mentioning that this woman was possibly someone we went to school with. So, I figured if this was the same person, that if anyone knew her, then Malcolm did. Just asking."

"Yeah, well, that's not something you would only ask. So, I'm going to say this and then leave it alone. Be careful, and like I said before, leave the past in the past. Don't go digging for something that could come back and bite you in the ass."

He took CJ from me and went into the nursery. Although I completely agreed with my husband about leaving the past in the past, my spirit just wouldn't let me. I was even more intrigued now than before to learn more about this Eva woman and Malcolm's dealing with her. After finding that we went to high school with her, their dealings had to be way more than we could ever imagine.

While Cedric was with the baby, I did a little reminiscing. So I went into our basement storage area, where we kept all our keepsakes. I knew exactly what I was looking for and where it was. The second I spotted my high school yearbooks, I sat on our sofa and searched for Eva. I didn't have a last name, but I planned on going through every photo until I located her.

After examining teenage photos for about forty-five minutes, everyone pretty much started to look alike, even the people I'd grown up with. I laughed at our hairstyles, clothing, and especially how my closest friends and I thought we were everything back then. There was no denying that we were the prettiest girls running through the school, and every boy chased us every second they could. Except for Malcolm, that was. He never did the chasing because all the girls flocked to him.

I looked at his pictures throughout the book from back then, and my heart practically skipped a beat. I hated that I was so in love with him back then and even more than he knew. He was right that everyone knew except for Cedric. That's when I ran across his picture. Cedric was not the person I thought I would spend the rest of my life with. He didn't play sports, wasn't considered popular, and wasn't someone the girls went crazy over. He was simply Cedric—funny, entertaining, class clown Cedric. And that was what ended up drawing me to him. He sat next to me on the bus one day, and I think I laughed the entire ride home. Ever since that day, not one second with him had been dull, and I'd been laughing with him ever since. Yet, I couldn't stop thinking about or wondering how different things would be if Malcolm were my husband instead of Cedric.

I almost called it quits looking for Eva after making it to the letter *S,* and still, there was no sign of her. At least, that was until my eyes hit the name . . . Eva Tucker.

"Oh my goodness. This has to be her. It's the same complexion, lips, and nose. I wouldn't forget those eyes from anywhere. Malcolm Carter, have you been with this girl since high school?"

That was the very question roaming through my mind and what I was determined to find the answer to. I was lost in thought . . . until Cedric's voice snapped me out of it.

"Baby, baby, are you cooking dinner tonight, or are you ordering takeout?" he asked as his eyes looked at all the books beside me. "You're down here looking through our yearbooks. You're looking for Eva, aren't you? Damn, Crystal, you just can't leave well enough alone."

He hadn't given me a chance to respond to anything. He simply shot me a dirty look and headed right back upstairs. I knew then that we were definitely going to have another night just like last night. However, this time, I was sure it would be me on the couch, and part of me didn't mind one bit. At least that way, I could give my body the satisfaction it desired while dreaming of the man I truly wanted. The man that could make me come without even touching me.

Chapter 15

Malcolm

My head was going in circles with all that had happened today. From Crystal seeing me with Eva at the coffee shop to Eva claiming she was pregnant, to wondering what Crystal might have told Mariah before I'd walked in, and now, Mariah telling me that she could never give me a child. It was too much. All I wanted was to sit back in my study and figure out things. So, I asked Mariah if we could stay home for dinner, and she agreed. Right after that, she headed to the bathroom to bathe, and I was sure she was out cold by now.

As I sat there thinking about my next move with all three women, my cell phone lit up on my desk. Just as I thought, it was Eva shooting me a text.

Hi, Malcolm, can you talk?

Instead of texting her back, I decided to give her a call. True enough, I was taking a huge chance of Mariah walking in at any moment, but if she did, I would only say that it was Cedric and hurry into the bathroom and close the door behind me like I always did. However, seeing that there was a possibility that I would have a whole child with the woman, I felt it was more than fitting to call her.

"Hello?" she answered. Her voice sounded peaceful and angelic like in the past, and I liked it.

"Hey, Eva."

"Malcolm, listen, I didn't like how we ended things earlier. I needed you to know that no matter how it seemed or what you were thinking, I didn't tell you about my pregnancy simply to keep you in my life. I mean, of course, I love you and want to be with you, Malcolm, but I'm also tired of all the secrecy between us from back then and even now."

"I'm trying my best to understand why you did what you did back then, but it's hard, Eva. You've had opportunity after opportunity to tell me the truth over the years, but you didn't. Instead, you withheld it from me and only said something now because I said we couldn't see each other again. Why would you do something like that, and how am I supposed to forgive you and move on?"

"I did it because I love you and didn't want you to leave me. I thought if I told you that I'd kept you from knowing we would have had a child together, you would walk away from me. But you're doing that now anyway, and I realize it's not about me anymore. It's about this child growing inside of me. This innocent child will symbolize the love we've shared all these years. This child will deserve two parents who love each other and them unconditionally. I don't want to take that from our baby. So that's the reason I said something now."

The phone grew silent. I assumed because neither of us knew what to say . . . until she asked, "So, now what, Malcolm? Where do we go from here?"

"Listen, it's going to take some time for me to forgive everything you've done, but if you're truly pregnant with my child, I don't want this baby to have to pay the price for our mistakes with each other. So just let me figure things out from here, and I'll take care of everything. But I'm asking you, Eva, no more shenanigans like last night or this morning. I need you to lie low and give me time and space. I need to play my cards right because if I don't, I will definitely lose everything."

"I hear you, Malcolm, and okay. I'll back off. But there's one other thing you should know. Your wife's friend, Crystal, approached me after you left earlier. She tried to act like she'd seen you from afar and recognized you from high school."

"What? What did you say? Did she recognize you from school?"

"Calm down, all right? I don't think she remembered me at all. At least, I didn't get that impression. So anyway, I told her that you were my attorney and I was a client. But somehow, she knows my name."

"How in the world would she know your name if she didn't know who you were?"

"I don't know, Malcolm. Maybe she heard you say it or something while we were on the phone."

"But there was no way. I was inside her husband's media room with the door closed, and the rest were in the living room. There was no way she could hear the call unless . . . wait . . . that had to be it."

"What? What's it?"

"I remember when I came out of the media room, she was coming out of the baby's nursery. That's it—the baby monitor. I bet you there was a damn baby monitor in the room, and she listened to my entire conversation with you. That's how she knew where we would be today and what time. Dammit," I said, pissed that I didn't catch on that night at their home.

"Well, like I said, just relax because I don't think we'll have to worry about her anymore."

"What is that supposed to mean?"

"It means that I took care of everything, and she won't be a problem for us any longer."

"Damn, Eva, what did you do?"

"Exactly what I needed to do to make her keep her mouth shut. So, don't worry. I handled it."

Her last words made me fearful. I didn't know what she meant by she "handled it," but it didn't sound right, and something told me whatever it was might backfire on us. I'd known Crystal just as long as I'd known Eva, and I knew she could be sneaky and conniving, which was the very last thing that I needed in my life at that moment.

"Eva, I gotta go," was all I could manage to get out before disconnecting the call. I didn't want to talk about or think about any of the women in my life anymore. It was all one big, tangled web, and I had no clue how I would claw my way out of it, especially without losing everything to my name.

Looking down at my phone, I realized I couldn't take the chance of Eva keeping her word. She was way too emotional and anxious for me to give her some answer regarding this pregnancy that I wasn't even sure was real yet. So with that in mind, instead of taking the phone with me into the bedroom, I put it inside my desk drawer for safekeeping until morning. Then I turned out the lights in my study and went into our master suite to shower so I could finally crawl into the bed with my wife and hold her for the rest of the night.

That's precisely what was on my mind, but it seemed something different was on hers. I heard her voice as I put my arm around her waist and spooned her close to me. It was soft and sweet.

"Malcolm?"

"Yes, baby—"

"Please, don't ever leave me. Don't give up on us having a family. I promise I will give you a child if it's the last thing I do." I felt a tear drop onto my arm.

"Sweetie, I already told you I am happy and totally complete with you. We never have to have children, and I would still be all right. I love you, Mariah, and I promise I will never leave you."

She scooted her rear closer to me, and I held her as tightly as possible. Her skin was soft, her hair smelled sweet like fruit and berries, and her body was warm. Mariah was everything I needed and more, so I knew I needed to be completely honest with her. So, a few minutes later, contemplating the inevitable, I asked, "Baby, are you still awake?"

"Yeah."

"There's something I need to tell you," I said as she turned to face me. "I don't really know how to say this. I don't even know how true it is, but—"

"But what, Malcolm? What is it?"

"There may be a woman from my past . . . she, um . . . um . . . She's claiming some completely untrue things and, well, I'm not sure how far she'll go to try to trap me up."

At first, Mariah hadn't said anything, but I could hear her gasp a little and see panic and fear inside her big brown eyes.

"Claiming some things like what, Malcolm?" She sat up and stared at me, waiting for an answer. I took a deep breath before responding, trying to decide if I truly wanted to be completely honest with her.

"She claiming to be pregnant, Mariah."

"Pregnant?" she repeated between breaths, seeming like that one word had taken all the air out of her.

"But I don't understand. We've been married for almost ten years and dated before that. Are you trying to tell me that you had an affair or something?"

"No, no, it was nothing like that, baby," I said, unable to tell her the truth of my infidelity throughout our entire marriage. "The truth is, I ran into someone from high school. We were intimate once, right before I left for college. Baby, I never spoke to her again after that, and it was what it was. But then I saw her again not long ago and, and—"

"And what, Malcolm? You saw her, and *what?*"

"I'd . . . we'd—"

"You had sex with her."

Seeing the expression on her face, I couldn't seem to let the words come from my mouth. So instead, I nodded my head in acknowledgment to confirm what she said.

"Anyway, when I saw her today, she told me she was pregnant with my child. But, baby, I don't know how true it is. I mean, we were only together that once. She doesn't look pregnant one bit, and I got a feeling that she's only saying this because she knows how much money she could come into if she had my child."

Mariah crawled out of bed and began to walk around with tears flowing freely from her eyes. "So, your meeting today was not a business meeting. You met with a woman you've been cheating on me with who claims to be carrying your child. You let me pour my heart out to you in that kitchen about never being able to have your baby when the whole time, there's some woman out there about to give you the one thing that I can't," she screamed at the top of her lungs.

I jumped out of bed and ran over to her, trying to hold her in my arms.

"Baby, baby, baby, please, listen to me. I have not been cheating on you the way you're thinking. Baby, it was only once, and that was it. I promise. And I'm telling you, I don't believe this whole pregnancy story, but I didn't want to keep it from you just in case it is true. But I promise, the woman doesn't appear to be carrying a baby. I mean, you can even ask your friend. . . . She saw me at the coffee shop with the woman."

"Crystal? *She* saw you with this woman?" She pushed me off her with all her might.

"Yeah. She saw me and the woman there together."

"She never said anything to me about it while she was here. So, now I know that's what she wanted to tell me before you walked in. It all makes complete sense now," she said, sitting back on the bed. "But, Malcolm, who is this woman? And what does she want? Is she asking for child support? Does she want you, her, and this baby to be one big happy family? Does she know that you've been married . . . for almost *ten* years?"

"Baby, whoa, slow down, all right?" I sat next to her and tried holding her hand. "To answer your questions, her name is Eva, and we went to high school together. We became friends maybe my junior or senior year. I can't quite remember. Anyway, she was awkward and quiet, so I befriended her just to make her feel good. Then like I said, I slipped up, and we were together once in high school. I don't even know why other than I was a teenage boy in heat running around with any girl that I could. But we recently came in contact again."

"And you just couldn't help yourself, right? Our marriage didn't mean enough to you to keep your damn dick inside of your pants."

"All right, I deserve that, Mariah. But being with her had nothing to do with my love for you. I'm not unhappy in our marriage and don't desire to be with anyone else. It just happened. It was a dumb, stupid mistake that simply just happened, and I wish I could take it back. But I can't, and you and I have never lied to each other, so I knew I needed to tell you.

"Anyway, I don't think she wants anything from me if you're worried about that. At least she didn't mention it. Instead, she said she wanted me to know she was carrying my child. So, I asked her if she had proof that she was pregnant and that I would need confirmation that I was indeed the father. So, that's the whole story. I didn't want to bring it up until I had a blood test or something done. But, Mariah, I needed to be honest with you. We don't keep secrets from each other, and I couldn't start now.

"Before I left the coffee shop, I told her we would need a paternity test once the child was born. She said she wasn't sure if she wanted to take her child through any of that. She said they would be fine with or without me and just needed me to know. So, baby, if she's not pressing the issue, neither will I. I will leave things right where they are, but there's my truth and transparency. I just wanted to be honest with you."

"Really? And that's it? But don't you want to know, Malcolm? I mean, if this *is* your child, don't you want to be in their life? A child needs their father. Besides, what kind of man would you be to know there's a possibility that you have a child out there, and you don't do what you have to do to find out the truth?"

"Listen, baby, I hear you, but if she doesn't want a test, then I won't push it. My family is with you, and that's it. So, I'm praying that today is the first and last day I will hear from her. All I want is for you and me to be like we've always been, loving each other with no secrets. And if and when I even hear from Eva again, then you and I will deal with it together at that time, all right?"

I pulled her back to lie down and put my arms around her. I had tried to say enough to explain being in Starbucks with Eva if anyone saw us and even brought up Crystal to cover all my tracks. Now that I believed I had handled everything with my wife, I needed to figure out things with my unborn child's mother. No matter what, I would not lose everything I'd worked hard for all my life. Not for anyone.

Chapter 16

Mariah

There was no sign of sleep in sight for me. Lying there in my husband's arms, I kept trying to close my eyes and find rest, but it wasn't trying to find me. I didn't know if it was more from the news I'd received from Dr. Taylor, the fact that my husband was possibly having a child with someone else, or that my best friend hadn't said a word about seeing Malcolm with another woman after what I'd shared with her yesterday. My heart was torn into pieces, and all I did was lie there with tears flowing from my eyes. I kept wondering what to do next. Should I leave my husband of almost ten years for one night of infidelity? Should I stay and make his life a living hell? Or should we seek counseling so that I could find out what possessed him to be with this woman? Not one answer was clear to me, and I was torturing myself more than anything.

After thirty minutes of tossing, turning, and watching Malcolm peacefully sleep as if he hadn't just admitted to cheating on me, I crawled out of bed to leave him to his slumber. First, I entered the kitchen to get myself a glass of water. Then I went into our living room and flipped through the channels on our flat-screen television. When that didn't cure my anxiety, I turned it off and walked toward Malcolm's study. I couldn't help but wonder about this woman named Eva, and I knew I wouldn't rest until I learned more about her. My mind traveled from what she looked like, if her unborn child indeed was Malcolm's, whether she was happily married, or if she hoped to rekindle things with my husband one day. Then most of all, I questioned if she was the very woman behind the mysterious scent. If so, that possibly meant that my husband's confession was a huge lie because there was no way I'd smelled it for the past two months if they'd only been together once. There were so many unanswered questions that I needed to uncover before I could fully get rest or trust my husband unconditionally again.

First of all, I needed to see her, just for myself. I needed to see her face, look into her eyes, and find any kind of truth and integrity behind them. I wasn't sure how to find her because all I knew was her first name and that she had gone to high school with him. But if I did nothing else, I was determined to find the woman claiming to have my husband's child inside her. I had to know if it was truly his baby and where we would go from there.

Turning on Malcolm's laptop, I went directly to Google and keyed in the name of his high school. After that, I searched for the years he attended and then searched for the name Eva. Immediately, a photo of a young girl came up. She was as plain as plain could be. She was extremely dark, with both soft and bold features on her face. Her lips were plump and pouty-like, and her nose appeared small with a protruding tip. But it was her eyes that stood out the most to me. They were large and piercing, yet dark and cold. There was a hint of mystery behind them, and I couldn't trace any sense of warmth and love within them.

"Is this you, Eva? What did you ever see in her, Malcolm? What exactly drew you to this girl?"

Never in my life did I consider myself an insecure woman, and as much as I wanted to stop, I couldn't. Even though Malcolm told me they'd only been together once since high school, I still had to go further to see if I could find who she was. I needed to see her for myself. The name under the photo was Eva Tucker, so I keyed that exact name into Google and hit the return button. Instantly, several pictures of the same woman showed on the screen.

"Oh my God." Although she looked drastically different from the younger version of the girl in the high school photo, I knew it was her. It was that exact same look in her eyes that had confirmed her identity. However, as a grown woman, she had turned out far more beautiful than that plain-Jane little girl from her childhood. She was breathtaking, and instantly, I understood the attraction my husband had toward her.

"Okay, calm down, Mariah. Just calm down. A woman as beautiful as she is must be married. She's not trying to have a family with your husband," I coached myself.

After looking at the picture a million times and trying to find something or anything undesirable in her, I finally gave up. I decided to go to the state's web page to look up marriages, divorces, and any judgments under her name within the court system. I searched her name there, but no marriage or divorce decree came up. That's when I found myself sitting there for the next thirty minutes, meditating on what I should do, until it came to me that I had no other choice.

Entering the words *White Pages* into the search bar to find an address, I tried to map out a plan in my head. It returned three possible addresses that I decided to write down. Of course, I hadn't concluded if I would go to every address looking for her, but at that moment, that was the only thing in the front of my mind. I wanted to look this woman who was claiming to have my husband's child in her womb dead in her eyes to find out exactly what she wanted.

I opened the desk drawer to grab a pen and tablet of paper when I saw Malcolm's cell phone lying there, staring back at me. I knew my husband better than he knew himself. He'd never let his cell phone out of sight, especially overnight. He lived by having that phone available to him every morning to check the day's news, weather, and other important information.

"What is really going on, Malcolm Carter? Why would you leave your phone in this desk drawer, and what more are you trying to hide from me?"

Picking it up, I no longer cared about his privacy. I entered his password to see exactly what I could find. The minute I keyed in the last letter of my name, which had been his password since we married, I immediately stared at one lonely text displayed on his screen.

Malcolm, what are we going to do about this pregnancy? Ms. Eva Tucker had sent it, and although he'd already told me about their one-time affair, it was like I'd just found out all over again. After seeing the text, I looked for pictures of her in his phone or anything to see if they'd established a bond. Nothing showed other than his call list, with tons of incoming and outgoing calls between them. That was the very moment I knew in my heart that there was much more than the "one time" my husband was trying to force me to believe. Letting my emotions get the best of me, without thinking, I pressed the number and put the phone up to my ear.

"Malcolm? I've been praying since we talked that you would call me back tonight," she said.

At first, there was nothing but air as I took in the unknown woman's words. Then I spoke very matter-of-factly to her. "This isn't Malcolm. This is his wife," I returned, noticing the sudden silence that attacked the phone for several minutes before she spoke again.

"Oh, um-um—"

"Your name is Eva, right?" I asked.

"Yes."

"So, let me ask you, are you *really* pregnant with my husband's child, or is this all some tactic of yours to be with your high school crush?"

"Ma'am, I—"

"Oh, now I'm 'ma'am,' huh? So *now* you have respect for me? I mean, were you respectfully thinking of me when you were sleeping with my husband?"

"I honestly don't know what you want me to say right now."

"I just want you to tell me the truth. I need to know for myself, and I need to hear it directly from you. Is the child you're carrying truly Malcolm's?"

"Okay." I could hear her taking a breath. I assumed she was thinking of what to say. "Yes, I told Malcolm I am pregnant with his child."

"And how far along are you?"

"About twelve weeks, but I hadn't told him until now. I was trying to figure out the best thing to do. I didn't want to mess up my child's future or Malcolm's."

"I see. And now? I mean, you must have some reason for telling him now after discovering you're three months along."

"Look, I told him because it was time. Nothing more and nothing less. I didn't want to keep this from him the way I did all those years ago. Malcolm deserved to know that he would have a child soon."

We'd both become silent once again before the words that neither of us would have ever expected came out of my mouth.

"Eva, I need to see you . . . woman-to-woman . . . face-to-face."

"What?"

"Look, I know this might sound a bit crazy, and honestly, I haven't thought everything through myself, but I need to see you, and we need to talk about what will happen from here."

"What exactly do you mean, 'what will happen from here'? I'm going to have my child with or without Malcolm's help. That's it. And Malcolm can either be in our lives or not. It's his call, and it's just that simple."

"I understand, and I would feel the same way if I were in your position. But if you claim this baby is Malcolm's, it's *not* just his call. It's *all* our call, and first, we will need a paternity test. Then *maybe* you and I can somehow find some common ground. Maybe we can help each other."

"Help each other how?"

"Well, that's something that we'll discuss face-to-face, okay? And, Eva, just so we're clear, my husband is to never know about this call, our meeting, or anything you and I have discussed. This remains between you and me."

"All right, wait a minute. Just let me understand. You want a paternity test to confirm that my baby is Malcolm's. And after that, you want me to agree to help you with something that Malcolm isn't going to know anything about? Do I have that straight?"

"Basically, yes. Eva, I figure that what's done is done. I can't do anything about the fact that my husband slept with you and conceived a child. But I can do something about how we move forward. So, either you can be with me or against me, but if you go against me, it won't be beneficial for you . . . or your child."

"Listen, I'm sorry, but I can't. I'm not totally sure I'm comfortable with all of this, not even talking to you right now. Whatever you have in your mind about how this is supposed to play out, I think we need to involve Malcolm."

"No, we don't, at least not right now. We'll involve him, trust me, but it has to be how I would like it at the right time. And to make you feel a little more comfortable and surer about everything, Eva, I'm willing to pay you $25,000 for your help—and to keep your mouth shut."

"Twenty-five thousand dollars? To keep my mouth closed about something I'm not fully aware of yet?" she questioned as her tone changed, and I could hear a slight chuckle behind her words. "Maybe that would be more than enough money for the average female, but nothing about me is average. I know Malcolm, his background, and where he came from. His family is very well-off, and he's a successful millionaire lawyer with a wife who's also successful in her own right. And before you ask, yes, I've done my digging on both of you. So, $25,000, unfortunately, would be like a penny in a bucket for me."

"Okay, then what about $100,000?" I challenged her. "Does that better suit a woman like yourself, Eva?"

"Listen, why don't you add a few zeros to that twenty-five thousand and make it two hundred and fifty thousand, and maybe . . . just maybe we can talk from there."

I gave her proposition some quick thought before I agreed. "Okay. I'll have an attorney draw up some paperwork first thing in the morning. And let's say we'll get together in the afternoon around three. I will text you the location about an hour or so before and no sooner. Then I will give you more information about what I would like after we confirm paternity. Agreed?"

She hesitated, and then slowly but surely, the magic word came from her mouth. "Agreed."

I immediately hung up and deleted the call from his call list.

"Mariah, what the hell have you done?" I asked myself while breathing deeply and hoping I hadn't bitten off far more than I could chew with this woman, or that my husband wouldn't know what I was up to until it was time. However, I felt relieved that I'd possibly found a way to give Malcolm what he wanted. Even if this affair of his wasn't what I would have ever wanted or expected, maybe it was my miracle in disguise.

Chapter 17

Eva

I bent over in relief the second we ended the call. Then I started pacing around my bedroom. My mind went in circles with what had just happened. I wanted to call Malcolm or even text him, but clearly, that wasn't possible now. She had his phone and would know of any communication between us.

"How on earth did she end up with your phone, Malcolm? You never detach yourself from that phone ever," I questioned as if he were standing in the room with me. Then I replayed our entire conversation in my head and tried to think of what to do next. I hated being caught off guard and unsure if I should go along with whatever she had in mind without Malcolm being aware of it.

"All right, she knows about the baby and wants a paternity test. I can do that. But after that, I don't have a clue about what she'll ask me to do. Yet, whatever it is, she's willing to cough up two hundred and fifty grand for it, and that will take care of me and this child for quite a while. But then what if that's just payment to keep us out of Malcolm's life for good? I can't do that. I can't keep my baby away from its father, no matter the amount of money."

My mind was so boggled that I fell back onto my bed in despair. "What are you going to, Eva? Take the money and run? Or maybe if I don't give in to her demands and I shoot back with some demands of my own, I could possibly end up getting more in the end. Maybe that's it. I'll play her game right along with her and get a bigger payoff than either of us expected. After all, *I'm* the one holding all the cards right inside my belly." I began rubbing my stomach, and a huge sense of relief rushed over me.

Instantly, I started to devise my own little plan in my mind to counter hers. I pulled my laptop that was sitting on my bed closer to me and looked up the rights of a biological child and its mother. First, I had to find out exactly what my baby and I would be entitled to regarding Malcolm. As my eyes rushed through hundreds of words and paragraph after paragraph, they finally landed on the wording I needed to see. It clearly stated that every child's right is to have their parents' physical, mental, emotional, and monetary support. And since Malcolm was much more financially stable than I was, our baby, along with me, deserved all of his support . . . and then some. I was overjoyed by the thought of beating his wife at her own game as I recalled her smug tone on the phone. However, I honestly hated having to do this to Malcolm. But deep down, I knew I had to do what was best for my child, especially not knowing what the wicked stepmother had up her sleeve. After a few more searches online about custody, child support, and even a child's rights in the event of its father's death, I learned that Malcolm would be worth far more dead than alive.

"Wow, little baby, you have turned out to be our meal ticket without even being born. If something were to happen to your father, we would inherit just as much of Malcolm's entire estate as that wife of his would, if not more." I talked to the fetus inside of my womb and could have sworn I felt it turning flips.

Suddenly, I thought about how drastically my life would change once this baby and I had Malcolm's fortune. *I* would finally be the one in a big, nice, fancy house with luxury cars at my disposal, designer clothes, shoes, and precious jewels. And most of all, *I* would be the one that birthed the heir to his throne. *Me*—the one his family and friends looked down on when I was younger. The one that wasn't worthy of being on Malcolm's arm back then, and the one that he'd really been in love with all these years. They would finally have to acknowledge me, and that thought felt damn good. Of course, I didn't want him dead or anything, but just knowing what my child would gain whenever that time did come was more than enough for me. I wanted to give my baby the life I didn't have, and I was going to do just that . . . by any means necessary.

Chapter 18

Malcolm

My eyes popped open at the regular time, and without really thinking, I reached over to the nightstand to grab my cell phone. After a few seconds, realizing it wasn't there, I started to panic and began patting my hand all over the bed in search of it. "What the hell?" I blurted out loud, wondering if my wife had taken my phone, when all at once it came back to me. "Damn. It's in the study."

At that very second, while still squinting, I allowed my feet to touch the bare, cold hardwood floor and walked toward my study. The entire time, I looked around for any trace of my wife, but she was nowhere to be found. Then, when I hit my study, still wiping my eyes, I opened my desk drawer to find my cell phone lying there just as I'd left it. "Oh, thank God."

However, as those words of solace spilled from my lips, my mind was puzzled because I could have sworn that I'd laid it face down when I placed it there. Yet, this morning, it was face up. With my heart racing in a panic, I instantly picked it up to make sure I didn't have any inappropriate texts from Eva, and to my surprise, there was nothing. There were no calls, texts, or anything from her, which seemed odd. She'd never done anything I asked of her, so it was a bit strange that she suddenly had. With that in mind, I sent her a quick text to see where her mind was.

Hey, good morning. How are you? was all that I asked, not wanting to elaborate any more than that. Then, attempting to calm down, I walked to the kitchen, since I could smell bacon and eggs. Once there, I found Mariah fully dressed and cooking breakfast, something she hadn't done for a while. I couldn't help but wonder what her motive was, especially after what I'd told her last night.

"Hey, you. Good morning," I said as cheerfully as I could.

"Well, good morning, sleepyhead," she shot back in the same tone, which was surprising and peculiar at the same time.

"You're up pretty early. How long have you been awake? Or did you get any sleep at all last night?"

"I got some. But then I went into the study for a little while and tried to do some work, and when that didn't help, I lay across the sofa to watch some TV until I dozed off. I didn't want to wake you since you were sleeping so soundly."

Whatever she'd said after saying she went into the study, I really didn't hear it. I was more focused on whether she was the reason my phone had been flipped over and whether she'd seen anything from Eva. I'd always been careful to delete messages after I read them and delete pictures and such, but with all that I had going on, I could have very well slipped up somewhere. However, if she wouldn't say anything, I certainly wasn't going to either.

"So, you decided to get up and cook this morning? This is something you haven't done in a while."

"I'm up because I'm meeting Crystal once she gets out of church. And I chose to cook this morning simply because I wanted to."

"Really? Okay, if that's the story you're sticking with," I said, grabbing a piece of bacon and putting it in my mouth to ensure I didn't say anything out of the way.

"Okay, honestly, does this have something to do with what you told me last night? In a way, yes, it does. I know that you said this thing with this woman only happened once and that I have nothing at all to worry about, but I don't know, Malcolm. The fact of the matter is you cheated on your wife, whether it was 'only once' or not. And now, there is another woman out there carrying your child. She has the one thing I just discovered that I can never give you, which bothers me a lot."

"And what? Breakfast is going to make up for that?" I slightly chuckled about it. "Baby, I said it last night, I said it way before last night, and I'm saying it again now. . . . The fact that we don't have children does not matter to me. You are my wife, and you're the only thing that matters. Now, I'm so sorry and apologetic for my infidelity. If I could take it back, trust me, I would. But since I can't, I need to deal with this like a man. I'll do whatever it takes to regain your unconditional love and trust. But when it comes to Eva and this baby, even if she proves that her child is mine, then we'll deal with it together at that time. Please don't let this upset you or destroy what we've shared for all these years."

"I hear you, Malcolm, but that's much easier said than done. You did the one thing that I would have never in a million years imagined you would do, and it's not going to take me a day or so to get past that. I need time."

"I understand. And the breakfast?"

"Well, I thought that maybe I needed to get back to what I used to do when we first got together . . . cooking and catering to you."

I saw the distant and pained look in my wife's eyes as those words came from her lips. As much as I tried to brush things off by saying it only happened once, I knew she was hurt and that I'd damaged what we shared. I knew then that I could never let her find out the truth that I'd cheated with Eva our entire marriage. So, I went behind her, putting my arms around her waist and laying my chin on her shoulder.

"Listen to me, Mariah. I'm sorry. I know that doesn't make up for things or make things any better, but I will say that every day from now on if I have to. You are a perfect woman and a perfect wife. No amount of cooking, catering, or anything else will change that. I was dumb and made a stupid mistake, and I hope you can forgive me, all right? Besides, we both know that cooking hasn't always been your forte anyway."

Finally, we both laughed together as I felt the tension in the room lighten just a little bit. Then I grabbed a plate and placed everything on it while nibbling little bites in between. "So, anyway, why are you and Crystal meeting up? You two just saw each other."

"Malcolm, do we really need a reason other than that's my best friend and we want to get together? Is that a problem with you?"

"No, it's not a problem. I just thought she'd be too busy taking care of her husband and newborn to be hanging out having girl time with you," I said, feeling that Crystal might have more up her sleeve than a simple girl's get-together.

"Honey, calm down, all right? We're only going to have some lunch at my favorite restaurant. I'm the one that asked her if we could get together, not the other way around. And if you need to know, I want to ask her to help me plan our ten-year anniversary party. It's a little over six months away, but that time will fly by."

"Mariah, now, you know I already asked you not to do anything elaborate. Of course, it's ten years, but I'd rather it just be you and I reflecting and looking back over everything we've been through and celebrating where we are. We don't need some big, fancy party to do that."

"Trust me, it won't be big and elaborate, okay? Just a few of our good friends will join us to celebrate our eternal love. And I just might have a bit of a surprise for you that night. Anyway, I gotta go, but enjoy your breakfast, and I'll see you later." She kissed my cheek, took her bag and keys off the island, and headed out the door.

"Surprise, huh, Mariah? Crystal or your time in my study last night better not have anything to do with this 'surprise.'"

As soon as I heard her truck pull out of the garage, I picked up my phone and checked for a return text from Eva, but still nothing. I couldn't lie that although I'd asked her to lie low and wait until I got back with her, it was bothering me that she wasn't responding. This whole baby thing was starting to get to me, and I hoped and prayed it wasn't true. I hoped it was only her way of trying to keep me in her life, even though a small part of me feared the worst. With that said, I decided to call her. Her phone rang and rang some more until I hung up and dialed again, only to get the same response.

"What the hell are you doing, Eva? If you won't answer your phone, maybe I need to pay you a visit. But before you, there's someone else I think I need to see first."

Chapter 19

Crystal

I wish I could've gotten more into the morning worship service, but whenever CJ wasn't being fussy, my mind had been solely on Eva. Last night, I did as much digging as possible to find out more about her. I wanted to see if she'd gone to college and where, where she worked, her family background, and everything. But nothing at all came up. The only thing I could find out was that it appeared she'd had a son years ago. On her Facebook page, she'd posted a poem written to her child, as well as a yearly tribute to him. However, it didn't say anything about what happened to the baby, and there was never any mention of the child's father, which was strange.

Of course, Cedric still had a lot to get off his chest about the fact that I looked her up, and I let him say what he needed to. However, his concerns weren't going to put a halt to my mission. When I brought this information to Mariah, I wanted to have all my ducks in a row because then, Malcolm would be unable to weasel his way out of any of it. Then and only then would my best friend finally see that she deserved so much more than him.

I buckled CJ inside his seat to leave and meet Mariah. Once I pulled off, I turned up the music and glided through the traffic. My thoughts raced from Eva to Mariah to Malcolm all in a matter of seconds but rested on Malcolm. I hated that I still felt the way I did about him after so many years, especially with such a wonderful husband like Cedric and with Mariah being my very best friend. But honestly, I couldn't help my feelings. Even though he had a way of driving me crazy, every part of me still desired the man. It also didn't help that every time I looked at my baby, it was like looking directly into Malcolm's eyes, which was starting to torture me. Luckily, Cedric hadn't noticed anything unusual, and I was determined to keep it that way.

Finally, pulling up to my destination, I parked the car in the lot and prepared to get CJ out of the backseat. However, before I could open my driver's-side door, I saw a very familiar vehicle speed right up in the space to the side of me. Quickly, my eyes followed him as he got out of his truck and into the passenger seat of my car. I didn't know what to do. My hands started to shake, and I felt goose bumps down my arms. Part of me wanted to try to alert someone or get out and run inside the restaurant, but I knew there was no way on earth that I could leave my child. No matter how long we'd known each other or whose best friend he was, if he was crazy enough to pop up like this and get inside my car uninvited, there was no telling what else he might do. So, swallowing the massive lump in my throat, I simply sat there quietly and waited for him to announce his reason for being there.

"Hey, Crystal," was all he said, like we were bosom buddies and like his behavior was normal.

"Malcolm, what are you doing here, and what do you want?" I asked, being sure to keep my hand near the horn.

"You can move your hand, first of all. There will be no need for you to blow your horn. I just need to know why you're following me around. I mean, even with me showing up out of the blue here today, it doesn't feel so good, huh?"

"Look, if you're talking about yesterday, I have a right to go to a coffee shop, Malcolm. And I can't help if you and some strange woman just happened to be there."

"Some strange woman, huh? Her name is Eva, and you know exactly who she is. We all went to high school with her, and now she's a client of mine. So, does that answer your questions about her, or is there anything else you need to know?"

"A client of yours? What kind of client, Malcolm? You mean more like your mistress ever since the day you and Mariah got married? It's funny how she's the same woman I saw you with that night almost ten years ago, and now I saw you with her again yesterday."

"Listen to me, Crystal, because I will only say this once. Stay the fuck out of my business, or there will be hell to pay. Now, you can think whatever the hell you want to think, but not a word of your thoughts better get back to my wife. If it does, Cedric will get an earful about how close you and I *really* became back in high school . . . and after."

"Are you threatening me, Malcolm Carter?"

"Of course not. Now, enjoy your lunch date with my wife," he said as he kissed me on the cheek and hopped out of the car just as quickly as he'd gotten in.

However, I couldn't let things end there because if he thought everything lay in the palm of his hands, then he was sadly mistaken. So,I let down my window and asked him, "By the way, Malcolm, does Mariah know that Eva's son is yours?"

Although I didn't know the truth to my question, I still asked just to rattle his nerves. I planned on discovering the truth to that just like I would his infidelity. However, instead of saying anything else, he winked his eye, threw his shades on, and got back into his truck. I sat there briefly, wondering what the hell I was going to do. I already had Eva threaten me; now, Malcolm, and who knew what was to come if he kept his word and told Cedric about what happened all those years ago . . . as well as not too long ago. Deep inside, I knew I needed to leave this alone, or it could destroy my whole world, but something just wouldn't let me, which scared me the most.

After sitting there and trying to regain my composure for a few moments, I finally summoned the courage to get out. I took CJ out of the car, walked in, and immediately spotted Mariah sitting in the far back of the dining room. There she was in a big floppy hat and sundress, sipping tea.

I loved my friend more than anything but hated who Malcolm had turned her into. She had to have the nicest of everything, whether it was her house, car, clothes, or shoes. Everything had to be name brand and super expensive, and, in my mind, very uncalled for. I remember when she was so down-to-earth and didn't need those things. Yet now, Malcolm had her believing they were basically nobodies without them. True enough, she had her own money and could buy whatever she wanted, but I still blamed him for her extravagant indulgences. More importantly, I blamed him for it not being me. *I* was the one who met him first, yet here I was, the one with the watered-down version of him and a mediocre life.

Thinking of Malcolm, I decided against telling Mariah anything about seeing him at the coffee shop yesterday or what happened today. I felt his lies and deceit would catch up with him soon enough, and he'd end up telling on himself without me having to say a word.

She must have noticed I was there because I saw her waving me over to the table.

"Hey, you." She got up and hugged me when I walked over and then took CJ out of his stroller and began cuddling and kissing him.

"Sorry to have you waiting here so long, girl. Church was a little longer than usual." I told a sweet white lie instead of telling her about her husband.

"It's no problem, and I haven't been here that long anyway. I had to meet up with my attorney before coming."

"Oh wow, I guess I always assumed that Malcolm handled all of you all's affairs."

"Not all of them, and especially not this because what I have in mind will surprise him."

"A surprise that you need an attorney for?"

"Yes, I know it sounds a bit weird, but you'll learn all about it soon enough. But I don't want to discuss it yet, so let's change the subject. Anyway, how was church service?"

"It was good. Well, at least the part that I was able to take in. CJ was a bit fussy today, so it was hard for me to concentrate."

"Not my CJ being fussy. He's a perfect little baby," she said, bouncing him on one knee. "Speaking of church, though, Crystal, I'm a little curious. Do you believe in miracles?"

"Of course I do. I think that's all a part of being a believer and having faith in God. But if you don't mind me asking, what's up with you suddenly asking about miracles? Are you trying to build your own relationship with God?"

"Maybe, I mean, I don't know. I guess so. That's one of the reasons I asked to meet you here today. Yesterday, I went to see my doctor, Crystal. She told me that I have fibroids and I need a hysterectomy."

"Oh no, Mariah." I touched her hand, which was free from holding the baby. "I'm so sorry. I know how much you wanted a baby of your own one day."

"You're right. More than anything, I wanted to give Malcolm a son."

"Speaking of Malcolm, how does he feel about all of this?" I asked, looking over my glass of water as I sipped.

"I don't know. It's hard to say with him. In one breath, he says he's okay if we never had children. But then, in another, he said we could look into adoption or something else if we truly wanted a child one day."

"And how do you feel about that?"

"I want whatever is best for our family, especially after last night. And no matter what Malcolm's mouth says, I know deep down that he wants a son. He's talked about having one pretty much since we married, but we've been waiting for the right time. I guess I just waited too long, and now, I can do nothing about it. However, Dr. Taylor said there are tons of other options if I can't have one naturally. That's when she asked about my belief in God. She said she believes in miracles and that God can do the impossible."

"And she's absolutely right, Mariah. You just never know why you might be going through all of this right now or what God can do if you only put your faith in Him."

"So, are you saying you don't think I should have the surgery? I should just trust and believe that having a baby can still happen naturally for me one day?"

"I didn't say that because the surgery might be something you actually need. What I am saying is to pray and trust God to give you the answer on whatever you should do. He won't steer you wrong."

"And what would you do if you were in my situation?"

"That's hard to say, Mariah, because this might be something that your health depends on."

"I know. But I keep asking myself, why me? Why did *I* have to have fibroids? Why did *I* have to be the one with the possibility of never having children?"

"Well, I think the question should be, why *not* you? Please don't mistake me. I would never wish any ill will on you, but we all have our own cross to bear, whatever that cross is in our lives, and this is yours. That's where your faith comes in. Maybe this is happening to draw you closer to God and deepen your relationship with him."

"Girl, you know that I'm nothing like you, okay? The closest I've been to going to church is attending a wedding or funeral. I don't know anything about going regularly and praising God to the high heavens like our mothers used to."

"All right, you don't know now, but you can always get to know him. God gives all of us a choice to choose him."

"Chile, you sound so holy right now that I want to pass the collection plate." We both fell out laughing while giving each other a high five.

Things got quiet for a second while I thought about everything I had just said to her. It was funny to me how we could always dish out the same advice to others that we needed to take ourselves. I mean, although I was in church Sunday after Sunday and loved God with all my heart, the minute I left, I was coveting my best friend's husband. Not to mention the other secrets that I had buried inside of me. I had no idea what Mariah was reflecting on, but suddenly, the waiter came over to take our drink and appetizer orders, snapping us both out of our daze. Then quickly after, Mariah asked the question I wasn't ready for.

"Crystal, why didn't you tell me that you and Malcolm ran into each other yesterday?"

I paused before responding, wondering if I should go ahead and be completely honest with her, especially since I'd just finished talking about God. I didn't want to seem contradictory, but it still wasn't the right time.

"Why would I tell you, Mariah?" I asked, looking around, wishing the waiter would come back. "I mean, he was in the coffee shop, and so was I, but I didn't think it was a big deal. Malcolm and I have run into each other plenty of times at other places before. Plus, we didn't even speak to each other yesterday." I tried to sound convincing through my nervousness since I didn't know what he'd said to her already. "Did he make a big deal about it or something?"

"Oh no, not at all. I just remembered that you and I talked yesterday and you hadn't said anything about running into him, but he, on the other hand, told me everything," she said in an odd manner, not making eye contact as I watched her put a little sugar into another glass of tea. I didn't know what she meant by he'd told her "everything," but I was positive that had to be far from the truth. There was no way on earth I could see him spilling everything about his true dealings with Eva.

"I'm sorry, Mariah. I guess it was something so small that it just slipped my mind altogether."

She stared at me long and hard, and her eyes almost said they didn't believe me. However, instead of continually trying to explain, I changed the subject and prayed she'd follow my lead.

"Anyway, your ten-year anniversary is only six or seven months away. Do you two have any special plans? Maybe a private getaway?"

Mariah giggled and blushed before answering, which told me that our previous topic, thankfully, was a thing of the past.

"No, no trips or anything, but I am trying to plan something special. Malcolm keeps saying he doesn't want anything big and elaborate, but it's ten whole years. Girl, many couples don't make it past three or what everyone calls the 'seven-year itch.' But our ten years have been good. Malcolm hasn't been running around with this woman or that woman, he's not a habitual liar, and I still feel just as safe, protected, and in love with him as day one. And I want to celebrate that," she declared, sounding more like a speech that she was trying to make herself believe than just a mere conversation with her best girlfriend. "Um, that's sort of where I need your help. I want to plan an intimate party with some of our closest friends, and it must be extremely nice and elegant."

"Okay, I guess I'm game. I'm sure we can come up with something."

"And, Crystal, just wait," she said, staring into space with a slight twinkle in her eye. "If all goes the way I plan, I will give Malcolm the surprise of his life."

I didn't have a clue what she was referring to, but whatever it was, knowing Mariah, it would surely be one for the books. My only wish was to expose him and Eva before then. That way, we were sure to be planning a divorce party instead of an anniversary party.

Chapter 20

Mariah

Thinking about my surprise for my anniversary, I immediately thought of Eva, which reminded me that I had to get Crystal out of here as quickly as possible. I didn't want her, Malcolm, or anyone else to know what I was up to before it was time. I'd texted Eva when Crystal first arrived about where to meet and when and knew she should be coming soon.

"Girl, listen, I'm sorry to cut things short, but I forgot that I told Malcolm I wouldn't be out long today. He wants to go to dinner this evening since I canceled last night, and it completely slipped my mind until now."

"Hey, no explanation needed. I think I will take my food to go, and the baby and I better get home to Cedric anyway."

"By the way, how is Cedric? I mean, since your disagreement with him and all."

"Girl, you know how it goes in marriage. Sometimes you need to agree to disagree to keep the peace, and I think that's what we both decided to do," she said while taking the baby from me and putting him inside his stroller.

"Well, I'm just glad that you two were able to work things out in your own little way."

"Yeah, me too, I guess."

"Can I ask you a quick question before you leave?"

"Uh, sure."

"Do you think Cedric would ever cheat on you? And if so, would you forgive him?"

"Mariah, why are you asking me something like that?"

"Girl, I'm just curious. I often wonder about it with so much temptation in the world and the fact that we have a couple of wonderful men as our husbands."

"Listen, I don't let myself think about things like that unless given a reason, and thankfully, Cedric hasn't given me one. But, if he had, honestly, yes, I would probably forgive him. We have too much invested for one mistake. However, if it was something like he'd cheated our entire marriage, then absolutely not. I couldn't and wouldn't forgive that."

"Yeah, same here, I guess," I said, not wanting to say any more than that. After that, we kissed each other on the cheek, and she and the baby left while I waited for my next lunch date to show. As I sat there, I couldn't help but think about how Crystal had lied straight to my face about seeing Malcolm yesterday. Not once had she mentioned Eva being there, which struck me as strange. As long as we'd been friends, I'd never known her to lie or keep anything from me, so why now was the question that lingered in my head. Maybe she thought that Eva really was a client or business associate. Or perhaps she didn't want me to be hurt by it. Either way, I knew that had it been the other way around, I would have definitely said something to her.

While caught up in my thoughts a few minutes later, I saw a tall, dark woman with tresses of coal-black hair walk in and look around. I wondered if I would know who she was when I saw her, but now that she was here, there was no denying it was her. She was beautiful and captivating. In fact, I almost started to feel a little insecure and didn't want her to know I was there. However, I sucked it up, swallowed my pride, and waved her over to the table. Slowly, I watched her walk over like a supermodel on a runway, and with every step, I felt smaller and smaller. Then there she was, standing directly in front of me.

"You must be Mariah?" she asked, and even her voice was beautiful. It was much more alluring than over the phone.

"Yes, and you must be Eva. Please have a seat."

She sat down and bypassed all pleasantries. Immediately, she asked, "So, what is it that you want me to do for you?"

"Wow, you didn't at least want to order something to drink or eat first?"

"No, I'm not here for all of that. I just want to know what you want from me, and what I need to do to secure the payment we discussed."

"Eva, look, you're making this seem so formal, and it's not. At least, it's not the way I want it to be. Now, I know this is awkward for both of us, but the thing is, I'm sure that my husband is more than likely the father of your child, and we are going to be family regardless of whether we want to. So, I would like for us to get to know each other and behave as such . . . a family, that is."

"So, if we're going to be behaving as a family, then why is Malcolm not here right now? Why can't he know about what's going on?"

"Malcolm isn't here because I know my husband, Eva. He's an attorney, and before anything else, he will want to get all the legalities out of the way. That's not how I want to approach this, though. I want to establish and build a relationship with you and your—I'm sorry, your and *Malcolm's* child."

"His name will be Malcolm Junior. If it's a boy, that is," she said, and her words practically stung me to the core—so much so that it was hard for me to speak.

"Um, and if it's a girl? Have you already decided on a name?"

"I was thinking about Madison for a girl."

"Wow, that is a beautiful name for a girl, and, Eva, I would love to build a relationship with you and Madison or Malcolm Junior. That is, after the paternity test is done, of course."

She sat there momentarily as if she were thinking about everything I said.

"Okay, and if I agree to all this, when exactly will you disperse the money?"

"Eva, don't worry, all right? This is not about the money, and as I said, I don't want things to be so formal. Once we have established paternity, trust me, you and the baby will be well cared for. But I was hoping that until then, you and I could establish a connection," I told her as I felt a tear creep down my face. "Eva, the thing is, Malcolm and I have been trying for quite some time to have our own child, but I just found out that won't be possible. Ever. I must have a hysterectomy."

"Oh, I'm so sorry. I had no idea," she said, and I was glad to see some sense of decency in her finally.

"Anyway, finding out about you and your baby was almost like a miracle to me, even though I'm not thrilled with how it happened."

"A miracle? What do you mean? In what way?"

"Eva, with this being Malcolm's child, I'm hoping you will allow me to go through this whole process with you. I'm talking about doctor's appointments, cravings, any birthing classes, picking out clothes, and even the birth. I want to experience all of it with you, and you won't have to worry about paying for anything. I will cover every-thing as well as give you the money we discussed. And I promise we'll tell Malcolm everything at the appropriate time. So, do we have an agreement?"

"Wow, you want me to give you an answer today? This is a lot to think about, and to be honest, I really don't like that we're not including Malcolm in this right from the start."

"Listen, I completely understand your hesitation, but, Eva, timing is everything. Now, if you allow me to control when my husband finds out things, that will be best for all involved, so please, just trust me on this. And I realize I just sprang all of this on you, so you're welcome to take all the time you need to think things over. But I promise, this will be a good thing for you, me, Malcolm, and most of all, the baby. We will be one big, happy family." I held up my glass of tea to cheer to the occasion, and hesitantly, she took the one glass of water that was sitting there.

"To family," I said.

"To family."

She and I talked a little longer, and the more we did, the more I had to admit that there was something about her that I liked. Of course, I still felt extremely nervous about this entire situation, especially about when Malcolm found out what I was up to. But I knew I was doing the right thing for Eva, her child, and, more importantly, my marriage. This way, my husband would still get what he'd always longed for, whether or not by me. That was exactly when it dawned on me that I was right regarding what I'd said to her. She really was my miracle, even if I didn't like it. I only wished this miracle didn't come with such a huge price tag attached.

Chapter 21

Malcolm

I almost felt bad about what I'd done to Crystal, but the truth was, she deserved it. She had been a thorn in my side for quite a long time, and now she was on the brink of ruining my marriage. The messed-up part about it was that I knew her concern had nothing to do with her friendship with Mariah. This was all about her and the fact that she still wanted to be with me.

I wasn't trying to be cocky or arrogant, but I knew precisely how Crystal felt. Ever since our sophomore year of high school, she'd had a huge crush on me, and it seemed like that crush hadn't diminished over the years. It was especially evident the night before her twenty-first birthday party. She, Cedric, a few of our other friends, and I had gone out for drinks as a pre-graduation celebration.

I could recall the entire night like it were yesterday as it played in my head. She was all dressed in white and looking as sexy as could be. I remember Cedric being incredibly proud that he had the hottest chick in the bar on his arm. However, all night, I found her watching me from across the room every chance she got. I played things off the best I could . . . one, because she was my best friend's girlfriend, and more importantly, *because* she was my best friend's girlfriend. That just wasn't how Cedric and I got down, and loyalty meant everything to us.

Toward the end of the night, Cedric had had a little too much to drink and wasn't sober enough to take her home. So, I ended up driving them both home, with her encouraging me to drop him off first. Against my better judgment, I did just that, and that's when it happened. She'd told me she wasn't ready to go home and begged for us to park somewhere near the water and watch the sunrise. I wasn't all that tired, so I agreed. So, there we were, sitting outside of my car, near the water, listening to music and drinking the last couple of beers I had in the trunk.

Then out of nowhere, her favorite song began to play on the radio. All I could remember was that it was something by New Edition. She began dancing and swaying to the rhythm of the music as I lay back on the blanket, and my eyes watched her body move like some sort of mermaid. I would have been a fool to say I wasn't turned on, but in the back of my mind was the fact that my best friend had trusted me with his girl. As she danced and swayed some more, the next thing I knew, she'd straddled the bottom portion of my body and began kissing me. I liked it, and to be totally honest, I liked it a lot, but not enough to betray my friend. So, I ended up pushing her off me and telling her to get in the car.

The entire ride to her house was silent. Once we arrived, she slammed my door and called me the biggest jerk she'd ever known. The next day, Cedric felt so horrible about the night before that he didn't even want to go to her birthday party. He figured she hated him for getting drunk and being unable to take her home. Anyway, I encouraged him to go and took him to get the biggest gift he could find. Although we'd gotten there pretty late, he still ended up looking like Prince Charming in her eyes while she blamed me for his tardiness. I didn't see any point in telling him the truth then or any time after, and she surely hadn't said a word herself—just like she hadn't said anything about what happened last year.

That night was cool and gloomy, and I remember the weatherman on my car stereo saying a bad storm was coming. Mariah had left for a business trip, and after working an extremely long day, I couldn't wait to get home, relax, and crash. So I picked up something to go, stopped to grab a bottle of my favorite bourbon, and headed home.

I could remember getting home and pouring myself a drink. I was about to shower when someone knocked on the door. It was Crystal, and I wondered what she was doing there. She knew that Mariah was away for the weekend, and what was even stranger was the fact that Cedric wasn't with her. From there, that's when things weren't so clear.

Quickly flashing right before my eyes were traces of my memory. Crystal claimed she didn't realize that was the weekend Mariah would be away. I walked into the kitchen to replenish my drink, and she asked if I would offer her one. After that, I woke up the following day feeling hungover or drugged with her about to leave. I could clearly recall asking her what happened, and her exact words were, "Malcolm, don't you remember? You said you wanted what should have happened the night before my birthday. But don't worry. Neither Mariah nor Cedric will ever know."

Although what occurred had been all of Crystal's doing, I didn't have the guts to tell Mariah about her best friend. So to this very day, it had been our little secret. But if Crystal knew what was good for her, she'd keep her nose out of my marriage, or both Cedric and Mariah would find out exactly what happened on *both* nights.

I had to turn my thoughts away from her and to some-one much more important. After leaving Crystal, I'd driven past Eva's home. I didn't see her car or any lights on inside, so I left. I'd been texting her ever since, and there was still no response. It was so unlike her usual behavior because she always answered me, and I was determined to find out what was going on. Since Mariah was still out, I figured I'd take advantage of the time I had to myself and give Eva a call. After the first three rings, I guess she wasn't going to answer again . . . until she finally picked up.

"Hello?" Her voice was sweet, and even after only about twenty-four hours, I'd missed the sound of it.

"Hey, I've been texting you like crazy. Where have you been?"

"You asked for time, remember? I want to give you as much time as you need. Plus, I've been thinking about things and how it's all playing out. I mean, you telling me that you want to be faithful to your wife, me telling you about the baby. . . . It all hit me that maybe it was supposed to happen this way. Maybe it is time for us to call it quits and for me to find someone who will love me and only me."

"And you came to this realization all in a few days? When you were just at my front door with me inside your mouth while my wife was sleeping?"

"All right, I admit that was fun, but I was wrong. And I wrapped my mind around the fact that I need to do better for this baby."

Although she sounded pretty convincing, I wasn't sure if I believed her or if she'd come to terms about everything so quickly.

"And speaking of the baby, what does this mean? I mean, we still need to have a test done and figure out how we will co-parent."

"Well, we don't have to go through with testing either. I mean, this baby is yours, Malcolm, but I don't want to go through having to prove that to you. I have loved you and only you ever since I was young. True enough, I didn't tell you when I was pregnant back then. I honestly thought I was doing right by you. But I've never once lied to you, and I don't have a reason to lie to you now. So, whether you believe I'm really pregnant or that the baby is yours is up to you. Either way, my child and I will be just fine."

"Are you serious right now? I mean, let me get this straight. You tell me that you're having my child only after I say we need to cut things off, and suddenly, you don't want me to be a part of your lives?"

"Malcolm, I didn't say I didn't want you a part of our lives. But sharing my child with you and your wife is not what I want. So, I'm doing the only thing I know to do and what would be best for everyone involved."

"Oh, so now you're doing what's best for everyone involved? After you've slept with a married man for years, now, suddenly, you have morals? And wife or not, if you think I'm going to have a son or daughter on this earth and not be in their life, then you have another think coming. I will die before I let my seed walk around and I not contribute to their life."

"Listen, I understand how you might feel, Malcolm, but as I said, it's truly what's best. And you can say whatever you want about my morals, but I wasn't sleeping with myself. So, just like you now have morals regarding your wife, I have them when it comes to being a mother to our child."

"What if you have a son, Eva? A boy needs a man in his life. How will you, as a single woman, raise him to be a man? I mean, what can you teach him?"

"Oh, so, do you think dropping by briefly to see him and me and then leaving to go home to your wife will teach him to be the man he needs to be?"

"It won't be that way, Eva. I can promise you that."

"Yeah, just like you promised me you would eventually leave your wife. Well, I've learned in just a couple of days not to trust in promises anymore."

"Listen to me good and clear, Eva. When that baby is born, we will have a paternity test done. And once it's proven that your child is mine, regardless of whether you believe me, everything will change."

I hung up before giving her a chance to say anything else. Although I didn't know yet if the baby was truly mine, I felt it and meant every word I said to her. I would die before not having a place in the child's life, especially since now it was the only biological child I'd ever have. A second later, she texted me using every foul word in the book. I almost played right along with her until Mariah came in the door.

"Hey, baby," she said quickly.

"Hey, sweetie." I pulled her close to me the minute she walked into the kitchen, laying my cell phone face down on the island. "How was time with Crystal today?" I asked while planting kisses all over her.

"It was good." She kissed me back in between her words. "We had a good lunch, I could love on CJ, and we started making a few plans for the anniversary party."

"You know what? At first, I was totally against this whole party idea, but the more you talk about it, I think I'm getting excited about it too. Even if it is more than six whole months away."

"Really? What changed your mind?" she asked with a huge smile plastered on her face.

"Seeing you happy and overjoyed that we've remained together after all this time means the world to me. Especially after what I told you. I am so sorry, and if having a party means this much to you, then I'm all for it."

"Oh, Malcolm, thank you, thank you, thank you." Then the roles reversed, and she began kissing all over me.

That was when it dawned on me that I had everything I'd ever wanted and needed right here with me. And with that thought, I tried not to focus on Eva and her child or what any damn doctor said.

"Baby, I've also been thinking about this whole baby situation." I held her a little longer before she walked away from me.

"What do you mean? What about it?"

"Well, I think we should follow our hearts and keep trying to have our own baby."

"So, wait. You're saying you don't want me to have the surgery?"

"Not a full hysterectomy. You said that the doctor offered other options, and I think we should look into those options. I want a child of my own, Mariah, not adoption or anything else."

"And what about the unborn child of the woman from high school?"

"I don't think we should worry about her. And who knows if she's truly being honest about everything anyway. I want a child with my wife and nobody else."

"Malcolm, I love you so much."

"I love you too, baby."

"So, do you think we can start now right away?"

"I'm following your lead, momma."

She took my hand and led me to the bedroom. I wasn't sure if I was doing the right thing by her, Eva, or even the baby. But one thing I was sure of . . . I wasn't about to lose my wife, my new son, or any of my wealth. Everything had to fall into place, or someone would pay—no matter who that someone was.

Chapter 22

Eva

I was furious after Malcolm hung up on me and knew it was time I took matters into my own hands. First, he utterly broke my heart by deciding not to see me anymore after promising for years that we would be together. Then his wife wanted me to join in on her master plan to give him the child she couldn't have. And now, he threatened to turn my baby's and my life upside down. Well, it was all too much, and I knew I had to continue devising my own plan to get what *I* wanted.

I hadn't thought everything through, but after meeting with Mariah, she seemed determined to be a part of my child's life. Sometimes, she even spoke as if my baby would be hers and Malcolm's, and I wouldn't be anywhere in the picture. However, I knew if I played her game right along with her, I'd have exactly what I wanted. My baby and I would have enough money at my disposal to have the life I'd always dreamed of, and then, eventually, we would disappear. So, with that in mind, I reached over and pulled my laptop close to me and Googled how to change your identity. Leaving the only place I'd always known as home wasn't what I wanted, but it was the only thing I could think to do to ensure my child's safety and keep it away from Mariah and Malcolm.

After about thirty minutes of studying the details on the internet, I pulled out the contract that Mariah had given me. Immediately, my eyes zoomed in on $250,000. I still couldn't believe she was willing to cough up that kind of money just to go to some doctor's appointments with me and experience everything I went through as if she were pregnant. But either way, I decided to go ahead and sign on the dotted line.

As I finished penning my signature, I must admit that I almost felt bad for her. She was a very beautiful woman and seemed extremely nice, and I could tell she was doing this simply to make Malcolm happy. Yet, she'd been married to a man who had cheated during their entire marriage, who had gotten another woman pregnant, and now only wanted to do right by her because of what he might lose. Although I still loved Malcolm dearly, I felt she didn't deserve what he'd done. Everything in my mind was a complete whirlwind, and I wasn't sure about any of it. The only thing I was positive about was that once I'd gotten the money, my baby and I would be long gone without any way for her or Malcolm to find us.

Six Months Later . . .

Chapter 23

Crystal

"Hello?" Mariah picked up on the first ring.

"Hey, girl, what's up? Are you free today? I thought we could run and grab some lunch and go over any last-minute details for the party. I mean, it's only a week away."

"Oh, Crystal, I really wish I could, but I have an appointment that I need to go to," she said in a hurry.

"Not another doctor's appointment? Is there something that you're not telling me? You've been going to the doctor quite often these last few months."

"I know, but I can't say just yet. Trust me, though, you all will find out soon enough."

"Mariah Carter, are you pregnant?"

"No, no, I'm not. But like I said, you'll find out everything soon, and believe me, I can't wait to tell you. Anyway, I gotta go. I'll talk to you later."

She hung up the phone before I could grill her any further. I couldn't help but wonder what my best friend was up to. For the past few months, she'd always been so preoccupied, extremely secretive, going to various doctor's appointments. I wanted to believe that whatever was going on, she'd trust me enough to at least share with me, but that seemed far from the case. Whatever her huge secret was, it was something I guess I'd have to find out whenever everyone else did.

When I hung up with her, Cedric came strolling through the door with CJ.

"Hey, sweetie." He walked right in, planting a huge kiss on my lips, and immediately handed the baby to me. "I didn't expect you to be home. I thought you were hanging out with Mariah today."

"We were, but she had a doctor's appointment. Anyway, how was your trip to your parents' house?" I asked while hugging my little bundle of joy as I followed Cedric into the kitchen.

"It was good. You already know my mother spoiled CJ every second she could while we were there. She also said she thinks he's beginning to take on some of her and my father's features."

"Really? Is that what she thinks?"

"Yeah, so I guess you and I aren't his parents, and they are." He laughed as the words came from his mouth.

He continued with his small talk, but I hadn't heard much. Instead, I looked down at my sweet baby and thought he was beginning to look less and less like me and more and more like his father. I couldn't help but wonder how much more his features would change.

"Yeah, well, I've always said that I think he has your mother's eyes," I said.

"I think so too." He stood next to me, both of us looking at this child we'd made. "I guess it's a little too late for me to deny him at this point, huh?" he joked, kissing the top of CJ's head and walking back into our family room.

As I stood in the kitchen cradling our baby, I thought about how much I had gone through to conceive him. Cedric and I had the hardest time getting pregnant. I wasn't sure if he or I was preventing it from happening. We tried everything the doctor, friends, family, and even the internet suggested. We'd both almost given up hope until one day, it just happened. We'd let go of all the pressure, and one evening, we shared a beautiful night of romance, love, and intimacy. Then, a little over a month later, we found out we were pregnant.

I remember Cedric being ecstatic and overjoyed that I could give him what I knew he always wanted. With that, I thought about how I would never let anyone destroy what I'd worked so hard for. Cedric, CJ, and I were one big, happy family, and if I had anything to do with it, it was going to remain that way . . . no matter who he looked like.

Chapter 24

Mariah

"How are you feeling?" I rushed into the doctor's office to find Eva sitting there looking as if she were about to burst at any second.

"I'm okay, I guess. But the pain is coming more often and much more intense than the last appointment."

"Oh my goodness, do you think this is it? Are we about to have a baby?"

"We?" she questioned with her face all twisted up.

"I'm sorry, Eva. I don't mean to be—"

"Look." She cut me off. "Please be quiet, all right? And I'm not trying to be rude to you or anything, but I'm in extreme pain, and sitting here with my child's father's wife is not making things any easier."

"I understand, and again, I apologize. I guess my excitement and enthusiasm are getting the best of me. I certainly don't mean to make you uncomfortable or more agitated than you already are. But, Eva, I really wish you would start looking at me as the baby's 'bonus mother' and not just Malcolm's wife."

She didn't say anything until a few minutes later when she cried out in pain. I knew there was no taking the pain away, so I tried doing the breathing exercises she'd learned in the classes. I found out quickly that she wasn't worried about breathing correctly. Her eyes said she wanted drugs and to kill me all at the same time. I'd hoped and prayed I could talk her into a natural birth, but she wasn't having it.

"Nurse, please put me in a room and give me something to stop this pain. Please. The contractions are coming every five to six minutes now."

The nurse came right over with a wheelchair and said she was about to call the doctor. When she said, "*I think it's time,*" my heart skipped several beats. I desperately wanted to call Malcolm and tell him to get here because we were having a baby, but I had to hold out just a few days longer. Our anniversary was only a week away, and then I could finally let the cat out of the bag. The second I followed the nurse into the room with Eva, she looked at me.

"Uh, Mariah, I know we had an agreement, and I signed a contract, but this doesn't feel right," she said through gritted teeth. "I really want Malcolm here."

"Eva, no, please. We are going to tell Malcolm, but not now. I understand he's the baby's father, and you'd much rather have him here than me, but please, just trust me on this. And as you said, you *did* sign a contract."

Before she could say another word, another contraction came right when my cell phone displayed Malcolm's name across the top. I struggled with whether to stay with her or possibly miss the baby's birth to take his call. Instead of answering, though, I decided to shoot him a text.

Hey, honey, I'm taking care of something right now. Be home soon.

Where are you, Mariah? Cedric mentioned something about you telling Crystal you had to go to the doctor. Why are you at the doctor's and why didn't you ask me to go with you? What's going on?

I knew good and well he wouldn't give this a rest and leave things alone until I'd given him a legitimate response. All I could think about was how I would strangle Crystal the minute this was over. Instead of texting him back, however, I decided to call since it seemed like Eva's contractions had calmed down. I stepped into the hallway and hit his number on the speed dial.

"Mariah, where are you?" he asked, all in a huff. "And what's going on? Why are you at the doctor's?"

"Malcolm, please calm down, all right? Honey, I've just been coming to the doctor about alternatives on us getting pregnant, that's all."

"So, why haven't you told me? You know I want to go through all of this with you."

"Baby, I know, but I don't want to get either of our hopes up until I know something will work."

"Are you sure that's all it is, Mariah?" His voice seemed to calm down.

"Honey, I'm positive. You will know everything at the right time."

Luckily, he didn't push any further. He'd said, "Okay, I love you, and see you when you get home," and that was it. As soon as I disconnected from him and returned to the room, the nurse handed me a paper gown, hat, and gloves.

"The doctor should be here any second," she said. "It's time for you two to have yourselves a baby."

I'd known for months that the nurse and doctor must have assumed that Eva and I were a lesbian couple. Neither one of us ever tried to correct their thoughts; one, because it wasn't anybody's business, and two, because it was much easier to explain being a lesbian couple than me being the wife of the man she'd had an affair with.

All at once, my mind began to have thoughts of my anniversary party next week when I was going to tell

Malcolm about the baby. I hoped that he would be just as ecstatic as I. In fact, I was sure he would. And finally, my little family would be complete—without Eva. Something inside had told me that she probably hadn't read the contract all the way through before signing. Little did she realize, after she gave birth today, that baby would belong to Malcolm and me. And after I'd announced at our anniversary party that she acted as our surrogate and birthed our child, she would no longer be needed. She could take that $250,000 she was so desperate to get and go on her own way.

Chapter 25

Eva

It had been six long months, and now I lay in this bed with various emotions. I went from being angry to scared, anxious, happy, to any other feeling. However, I wasn't sure if the anger was from the painful contractions or Mariah forcing herself on me and behaving as if it were *her* giving birth instead of me. So much of me wanted Malcolm here, standing right by my side and holding my hand instead of this wife of his. Having visions of him was the only thing that seemed to calm down my pain.

Although I hadn't talked to him in the past few months, it wasn't because I didn't want to. On the contrary, my heart was still with him, and as I carried our child, I wanted him more now than ever. I could visualize our family together in our big, fancy house with our dog and white picket fence, living the life I'd always dreamed of. But deep down, I knew that dream would never come true if I wanted to see any part of the money Mariah had promised me. Continuing to focus my thoughts on nothing other than Malcolm Carter, another contraction hit as the severe pain shot straight through me.

"Oh my God!" I screamed at the top of my lungs. "Please, make it stop."

"C'mon, Eva. Everything is all right. Just breathe through it. *We* can do this," I heard her say in her irritating voice.

"What the hell do you mean *we*? *I'm* the one having this baby—*not* you." I knew I'd hurt her feelings from the look on her face with what I'd just said, but I didn't care. What I said was absolutely true. It was *me* giving birth to Malcolm's child, not her, and I was tired of pretending. That said, after the nurse announced that I should be delivering soon, I decided to make an executive decision.

"Listen." I spoke between pain and deep breaths. "I know what we agreed, but I can't do this without Malcolm, so I think it's time that I called him. He will hate me if I give birth to his child and not have him here."

"No, no, Eva. Look, please, don't do this. As you said, we have an agreement, and now is just not the time to call my husband. I promise he will know everything at our anniversary party by next week, but not any sooner than that."

"Mariah, this is crazy. Please. I need Malcolm," I told her.

"You need him, or the money we came to terms with? I mean, it's your call. We can call off our whole arrangement, and I'll call Malcolm right now. But you know that will mean your forfeiting everything, and after this birth, you and your child will go back to exactly what you have . . . nothing."

I shot her the dirtiest look I could; if looks could kill, she would surely be dead. But knowing I was much more determined to get the money, I conceded and gave up any hopes of Malcolm being here. Yet, what she didn't realize was that I didn't plan to walk away so quickly once he knew the complete truth. By next week, the ball would be in Malcolm's court and no longer hers when it came to the future of my child and me.

Then, before I knew it, another contraction came as the doctor entered the room. He immediately threw on some gloves, checked to see if I was ready, and in a matter of seconds, told me to push. After at least five huge pushes and a ton of pain later, he laid a healthy baby boy on my chest, born at 7:17 and weighing in at seven pounds, nine ounces.

Looking at my baby, even at a few seconds old, he looked just like his father to me. His nose was Malcolm's, his hairline was Malcolm's, and even the way he squinched his little eyes was all Malcolm's. All at once, I kissed my little bundle of joy when I was suddenly reminded that we weren't alone.

"Eva, please, can I hold him? Please, give him to me," she said as a rush of tears flowed from her eyes with her arms outstretched.

"Uh, I'm sorry, Mariah, but I can't. I want to be the only one to hold him for at least the next twenty-four hours. I mean, other than the nurse, of course. I hope you understand."

"Eva, no, I don't understand," she said, wiping her tears away and snapping back into reality. "We have an agreement, and I'm the one who has paid for everything, including your giving birth in this expensive hospital. You owe me this much. Not to mention, I will be a mother to him once Malcolm finds out everything. So, please, just give me this one opportunity to hold him right now. You know I'll never get this chance again in life."

I truly felt her pain as she spoke, but I had to stick to my guns. And I didn't care what she'd done or paid for. That moment with my child was priceless, and it would be ours and ours alone. "I'm sorry, but the answer is still no, Mariah. Malcolm is *my* son, not yours, no matter our agreement."

"Wait. Did I hear you correctly? So you're naming him after Malcolm?" She stood there looking confused.

"Of course. His name is going to be Malcolm Isaiah Carter II."

"Eva, you can't. We never discussed this and haven't even had a paternity test done yet. Not to mention the fact that no one knows what the future may hold. I could possibly still have a child one day."

"Listen, I don't need a paternity test, all right? And believe me, I'm not doing this to hurt you. But this is Malcolm's son, his firstborn son, and regardless of whether you like it, his name will be Malcolm Carter. Now, if you don't mind, I would like you to leave. I really want this time alone with *my* baby."

Appearing totally defeated, she didn't say another word or put up any more fight. Instead, she grabbed her things from the chair in the corner and left as quickly as possible.

Once she was gone, I cradled little Malcolm in my arms, wondering what the hell I'd done. When all of this started, I was enticed by the money and the thought of getting back at Malcolm for shutting things down between us. But at that moment, while holding the most precious thing in my life in my arms, I was beginning to feel like I'd sold my soul—and baby—to the devil. Not to mention the fact that my heart had been longing for the only man I'd loved in my life. I felt horrible that he wasn't there to witness the birth of his only child.

So, before I knew it, I picked up the receiver of the hospital phone and dialed his cell number. I knew Mariah would likely be furious with me, but I didn't care anymore. Malcolm deserved to know that his child was born, and my son deserved to have his father there. After a few rings, I finally heard his voice on the other side.

"Hello? Hello?"

I desperately wanted to say something, but I couldn't allow the words to come from my mouth. All my mind was focused on was the money I was sure Mariah would deny me if I told Malcolm what she planned. That money would secure a future for my child and me, so I knew there was no turning back. I listened to Malcolm call out several times before I hung up.

"I hope you understand, my sweet baby, that Mommy had to do what was best for you. I'm only doing this because of how much I love you."

Chapter 26

Malcolm

The name on the caller ID read Christ Memorial Hospital. As weirdly as Mariah had been behaving lately, I couldn't help but wonder if it was her. Instantly, I called back and questioned the operator the second she answered.

"Christ Memorial."

"Uh, hello. I'm trying to find out if you have a patient there. My wife."

"What's the name, sir?"

"Mariah. Mariah Carter."

"Hold on for just a moment, please."

My heart started to race as I heard her tapping on the keys to her computer. Mariah had sounded fine when we spoke, but her behavior had been extremely strange and questionable for the past few months. She'd been secretive, leaving the house at all times of the day and night and constantly on her phone with someone. If I hadn't known better, I would have thought she was cheating, but that wasn't Mariah's MO. Something was going on with her, and I was determined to find out what that was. As the millions of questions went around and around in my head, the nurse returned a second later.

"Hello, sir? We don't have a Mariah Carter here in our hospital. Are you sure she was brought here?"

"Um, no, no, I'm not sure. But thank you so much for checking." I hung up, even more curious and suspicious than before I had called. "Where are you, Mariah, and what is going on with you? And if it wasn't you that called, then who did?"

I kept trying to put two and two together when it came to my wife until, out of nowhere, it hit me. Eva. I hadn't heard anything from her over the past few months. It was almost like she had vanished from the face of the earth. Although our last conversation hadn't gone very well, I'd tried calling and texting to make amends, but there was never a response. My heart wanted to let it go and direct all of my attention to Mariah, but knowing Eva was more than likely carrying my child and I wouldn't be a part of their lives had been tearing me up inside. What if she was pregnant, and what if she was in labor or something? Quickly, I pulled up the calendar on my cell phone and went back to the last time we'd spoken to one another. That was a little under six months ago. At that time, she was claiming to be around twelve weeks.

"Damn, it's been almost nine months. Was that you, Eva? But how in the hell did you afford Christ Memorial Hospital?"

I pulled up the number on my phone again and dialed out to put any questions to rest. The same nurse answered, sounding just as chipper as she had the first time. I hoped she wouldn't recognize my voice, first asking about my wife and now a whole other woman.

"Christ Memorial."

"Hi, um, I'm trying to find out if this is the hospital my cousin just had her baby at." I made up some bogus relationship.

"What's the name, sir?"

"Eva. Eva Tucker."

"Hold on, please."

I waited patiently for her to come back and give me the same response as before . . . until I heard the words on the other end of the line.

"Sir? Yes, Ms. Tucker is here, and I'll connect you to her room."

"Uh, no, that's okay, but thank you for your help."

I hung up and started pacing my living room floor. Most of me wanted to rush over there and be by her side, but a small part of me knew that would have been insane. I hadn't talked to her in the past six months *after* denying that she was being honest about being pregnant in the first place. How could I just walk in there ready to have a baby with her? Besides, there was no way I could explain things to Mariah either, or then again, maybe I could. I could tell her that Eva had the baby and wanted to do the paternity test as soon as possible. It sounded reasonable enough to me, so that was exactly what I would go with. I grabbed my keys off the coffee table and was ready to head out until Mariah suddenly came through the door. Immediately, I stopped in my tracks and looked at my wife, who wasn't herself at all. Her hair seemed somewhat disheveled, and she had a distant look in her bloodshot red and puffy eyes.

"Baby? What's wrong? Is everything okay?" I questioned as she walked right past me and straight toward our bedroom. "Mariah? Do you hear me?"

She almost appeared zombie-like, not saying a single word. Then I grabbed her and forced her to look at me once she reached the bedroom.

"Mariah, what is going on with you?"

"Nothing, Malcolm. Everything is fine. I just need some rest."

"Honey, you haven't been acting like yourself for months now. And look at you . . . your hair, your eyes. Talk to me and tell me what's going on."

"I've just been overwhelmed with everything these last few months," she said, tears beginning to drip from her eyes. "I mean, with trying to get pregnant, trying to get over the fact that another woman is having your child, and even with planning the anniversary party. It's all been a bit much. And yes, I've been crying so much today as I have so many other days, Malcolm. I'm afraid for the state of our marriage if I can never give you a child. I've been scared ever since you told me about your affair with this woman, and I don't know how to get past it."

"Baby, look," I said, moving her to the bed and sitting her down. "I told you. It wasn't an affair. It was the one time, and that's it, and I'm so very sorry. I promise you that it will never happen again. You can trust that. And, yeah, I know I suggested that you don't have the surgery and we still try to have a baby, but I don't want you to feel any pressure with that, Mariah. I told you before that I'm still fine with it if it never happened, and it won't change things between us. You are my wife, and you mean more to me than anything else in the world. And instead of having this party, why don't we go away? I can have our travel agent book us a trip somewhere exotic, six nights and seven days. What do you say?"

"No, Malcolm, we can't. This party means more to me than you'll ever know. If all goes as I have planned, our friends and family are going to witness something special that night, a miracle, and I can't wait to share it with them . . . or you."

"Mariah, what are you talking about? What do you have up your sleeve?"

"You'll just have to wait and see, honey. But my anniversary gift to you is going to change both of our lives forever," she said, getting up and going inside our bathroom.

I had no idea what Mariah was talking about, and for some strange reason, it made me uneasy. I had a week to find out what she was up to. So, once I heard the shower turn on, I grabbed her cell phone from her purse. She never kept it locked, so I hoped there were texts or something that could tell me what I needed to know. I looked at her text log, which looked like it had been wiped clean. I was sure she'd texted Crystal earlier that morning, and we'd sent several texts during the day, so why were they all gone? That was the question roaming through my mind. Then I went to her call log, which seemed pretty normal. There were calls from me, Crystal, her work, and a few other friends, but then I noticed an unknown number that wasn't labeled with a name. However, the number looked strangely familiar, and it appeared repeatedly.

"What the hell, Mariah? There's no way you've been communicating with Eva. So what is going on?"

I threw her phone down on the bed and made sure I had my keys. I was going to the one place that would give me all the answers I needed. Christ Memorial Hospital.

The 10-Year
Anniversary Party

Chapter 27

Crystal

"Baby, can you believe that in just a couple of hours, we are about to celebrate my best friend and your best friend being together for ten whole years?" he asked, touching up the lining in his hair in our bathroom mirror.

"Yeah, it is kind of surreal. I mean, who would have ever expected them to last as long as they have?" I said while applying lotion to my body.

"*Me*. I knew from day one that they were made for each other. Even when Malcolm was about to propose to Mariah, he asked me if I thought he was doing the right thing. Without hesitation, I said yes, without a doubt. And the rest is history."

"But what does it all mean if he hasn't been honest and faithful to her the entire time?"

I heard his trimmers shut off as he stepped into the bedroom and looked at me. "Crystal, please don't start, all right? This is our friends' special night, and they deserve as much love and support as we received from them on our anniversary."

"But you've never cheated on me, Cedric, especially not the night before our wedding and continually after."

"Baby, I thought you let all that go. What you're talking about is only an assumption. Mariah and Malcolm are extremely happy, to the point that they're trying to have a family of their own now. We should support them and not come up with crazy conspiracy theories."

"I'm sorry, Cedric. Maybe you're right, but something tells me there is much more to Malcolm and the woman I saw him with the night before their wedding. Honey, I think it's the same woman from high school. Eva. And I believe they may have been together this entire time."

"What? Girl, now you're *really* talking crazy, Crystal. That's insane," he said, laughing me off.

"Why? What would be so *insane* about it? And don't you find it strange that Malcolm suddenly wants a baby after all this time? When he's been saying forever that they don't necessarily need to have children? I seriously think that this whole baby business is only because he's just trying to cover up for something else, like a ten-year affair," I threw out.

"Listen." He walked over to me and placed his hands on my shoulders, looking me dead in the eyes. "Please, I'm asking you to be on your best behavior tonight and leave all your thoughts, assumptions, concerns, and conspiracy theories inside this bedroom. This is our friends' night. Let it be happy. And definitely don't let anything come out of your mouth to Mariah about Malcolm possibly being with another woman."

On that note, he went back inside the bathroom while I went to make sure CJ was still sleeping. For the past few months, I hadn't been able just to *let things go* the way Cedric wanted me to, especially not after this past week. After much Google and social media searching, I found *she* was possibly pregnant and had given birth to a baby boy. I'd seen a picture of her from her Facebook page, posing with a newborn baby. I couldn't help but wonder if it were Malcolm's, and if so, how he would explain things to Mariah. I even tried to find some link to another man who could be the father to tear down my suspicions.

Yet, there was nothing. Then there was the fact that both Malcolm and this Eva woman had threatened me. I knew without a doubt that there was no way they'd both be so on edge if they didn't have something to hide. My heart, mind, and gut told me that they were cheating and that her son was *their* son—*their* love child.

I'd been thinking for the past week about if and when I would share my concerns with Mariah, and how. Part of me feared what could happen if I went too far, but the other part didn't care one bit. Before it was all over, I would tell Mariah my suspicions and put the ball in her court. And Malcolm had better hope that he didn't say anything out of the way tonight or that time would come a lot sooner than any of us expected, and Mariah would surely get an earful.

Suddenly, I heard my phone buzzing where I'd left it in the kitchen. Once I made it there, I saw Mariah's name flashing across the front of it.

"Hello?"

"Hey, what time will you and Cedric make it here?"

"Mariah, the party doesn't start until eight, and it's just a little after six now. We'll be there on time. Is something wrong?"

"No, nothing's wrong," she said, but I detected something different in the sound in her voice. "I just need this night to go off without a hitch. Especially when it comes to my surprise for Malcolm."

"Yeah, this *major* surprise that I've only been waiting months to hear about. Spill it already. What is it?"

"I'm sorry, Crystal, but you're just going to have to find out with everyone else on this one."

"Not even a little hint for your best friend?"

"Look, all I can say is that this surprise will definitely change Malcolm's and my lives forever if everything happens the way I hope. We're finally going to have everything we ever wanted."

"Everything you ever wanted, huh? You know the suspense is killing me now, right, Mariah?"

"Don't worry. It won't be much longer."

Beyond my better judgment, I decided to ask, "So, where's Malcolm? Is he ready for the night?"

"I think so. He's been quiet and almost weird acting for the past week. I'm assuming he might be calculating the figures for this party in his head and trying to make sure I'm not going over budget."

"Oh, okay. Well, I hate to pry, but I have to ask. How has the baby making been going?"

"Uh, I guess you could say it's been okay. I mean, to be honest, we haven't been trying as much as when we first started, but I don't think either of us has given up hope. I just think we still have a long road ahead, and besides, my doctor believes that if it happens, it will happen when we least expect it. But to be honest, we may not even need to try so hard after tonight."

"Wait. What is that supposed to mean?"

"You know what? Maybe I've said too much, so I'll just see you and Cedric when you get here." She hung up, and I was much more dumbfounded than before the call.

"Mariah, what is going on with this surprise of yours?" I asked myself. From what I could gather from the minor details she'd already spilled out, I thought maybe she'd adopted a child without Malcolm or anyone else knowing. With that in mind, I put a lot more pep in my step to get ready and get there as quickly as possible. There was no telling how this night would end, and I planned on having a front-row seat to it all.

Chapter 28

Malcolm

For the past week, I couldn't focus on the anniversary party as much as Mariah probably would have liked. Instead, my mind had solely been on two things: the fact that I'd found Mariah had possibly been in contact with Eva and that Eva had likely given birth to our child. When I had left to go to the hospital a week ago, I'd made it to the parking lot but never inside. I knew that had I gone in and seen Eva and my child, my marriage to Mariah would be destroyed forever, and I couldn't take that chance. Reality sank in when I thought about losing everything I'd worked so hard for, and I wasn't about to let that happen.

Then there was that mysterious phone call. I hadn't heard from Eva anyway. I hoped that if she was genuinely pregnant and had given birth, I would be the first one she called, especially since she claimed I was the father. Yet, that hadn't happened, which made me question if anything she'd said had been the truth to begin with. I also couldn't get past the fact that she was at Christ Memorial, a hospital I knew good and well that she would never be able to afford. It wasn't making good sense, and I couldn't piece it together. However, at least for the rest of the night, I knew that I had to put my matters with Eva aside and put on a happy face for Mariah, who had just walked into my study.

"All right, baby," she said, holding three dresses up to me. "Which one do you think would be best? I love the black one the most, but I feel it might be a little cliché. I mean, everybody will expect me to wear a little black dress. But then there's this red one, which might be a little too much for our friends. And then there's this white one, which will make me look sweet, innocent, and angelic, but I don't know. What do you think?"

"Honey, I don't know. Haven't you already gone over your attire with Crystal?"

"I did, but I'm asking you which one *you* prefer. Crystal isn't my husband of ten years, Malcolm. You are," she said with a bit of attitude, and I knew I needed to ease up and play along.

"Well, since it looks like I won't get out of answering, I say go with the black. It's sexy, and I've always loved seeing you in a black dress."

"Okay, then, black it is. And when are you going to get dressed?"

"Baby, you drive me crazy when you get like this. I have more than enough time to get ready because guess what? The party is right here in our home."

"Whatever, Malcolm," she said, leaving, but I followed right behind her. There were some things I needed answers to before we acted as the perfect, happy couple all night.

"Baby, I went into one of our accounts and found a substantial amount of money withdrawn. Did you recently take out some cash?"

"Uh, of course I did. But you know that I've been planning this party for months, and I had a lot of things to cover."

"Yeah, but the amount of missing money is way more than what this party should have cost. I mean, it's not even like we had to pay for a venue because it's right here in our home."

"But I had to take care of the food, the ice sculpture, the band, the décor, and so much more, Malcolm. Trust me, okay? Besides, it's not like we don't have the money."

"That's not the point. You know I don't like spending money frivolously," I said, sitting on the bed.

"Malcolm, can you please stop worrying about the numbers right now and just try to have a good night? Please? Everything will work itself out."

"Yeah, if you say so, but I'm going over our account tomorrow with the accountant. I'm not in the business of just throwing money out the window like it grows on trees."

"I understand, Malcolm."

"And another thing. Are you sure your friend is going to play nice tonight? Other than bumping into her here and there when she's come to help you with the party, we haven't been around each other much. I don't want her nonsense all night."

"Everything will be fine, honey, if you also stay on your best behavior. I doubt if Crystal will act crazy with you if you're nice to her. Now, please, it would make me feel a lot better if you started getting dressed. The caterer will be here any minute, the photographer is already here, and you know a few of our friends will arrive early. I don't want them seeing you in your lounging attire."

"Okay, okay, okay, Mariah," I said, getting up from the bed with her giving me a little push toward our bathroom.

I had to be honest that this party would not have even taken place if I didn't love my wife as much as I did. We'd spent way too much money on it that we could have used to take a trip. And despite what she'd said, I know it didn't cost the amount of money that was gone from the account. She had some serious explaining to do the second this whole party was over. Then there was the small group of friends that were coming. Other than Cedric and

Crystal, none of them had been inside my home since we'd first married, and Mariah knew how I felt about others being inside our personal space. Finally, with everything going on in our personal life, I didn't feel like smiling and grinning with everyone all evening. Instead of continuing to focus on the negative, though, I tried to adjust my mood and hoped for the best.

Cedric's name scrolled across my phone as I was about to shower.

"Hey, Cedric, what's up?" I answered.

"Hey, man, I'm just checking on you and making sure you're ready for the big evening our wives have been planning for the past few months."

"Listen, man, I think I am as ready as I'm going to get, but I gotta be honest. I will be extremely happy when it's all over."

"Yeah, I bet. Uh, but I was actually calling for another reason too."

"What's up? Is something wrong?"

"No, nothing's wrong. But I was just wondering, do you remember a girl named Eva from high school?"

"Eva?" I started to get nervous at the mere mention of her name. "I vaguely remember her, but why are you asking?" I asked, wondering why he'd bring her up at such a random time.

"You know what? I probably shouldn't be saying anything, but for some crazy reason, Crystal seems to think she saw you two together the night before your wedding. Now, you know me. I'm your best friend and will have your back no matter what, but I just had to make sure. That's not true, is it?"

"Cedric, listen, I don't know what Crystal thought she might have seen that night, but no, she didn't see me at all with Eva Tucker from school. I was just as happy all those years ago as I am now with Mariah. Besides, you and I know that Eva had never been in our league."

"See? See? I kept telling Crystal that she had to be seeing things and coming up with craziness about you and Eva from high school. I didn't even remember you being friends with the girl in school, let alone having something going on with each other before you married. But look, man, I'm sorry, Malcolm. Please, forgive my wife's vivid imagination, all right? I'll take care of things with her from here now that I've talked to you about it."

"All right, I can respect that. But I do have one question, though. Has Crystal said why she has this bone to pick with me? Why I'm living rent-free in her mind?"

"Hey, I wouldn't go as far as to say you're living rent-free in her head. But the only thing I can come up with is the night before and the night of her birthday party. I honestly think she hasn't gotten over the fact that I'd gotten as drunk as I was the night before and then showed up late the night of the party. Like I said, I apologize. She can become a bit obsessed with something when she's focused on it."

"Well, maybe the three of us need to sit down one day and discuss both nights and let the chips fall where they may."

"I would hate to revisit the past, but if you think it might help, I'm all for it. I want her to let this go as much as you do."

"Okay, good. Well, on that note, I'll see you when the two of you arrive."

Cedric and I hung up, and I was furious. So much of me wanted to address things with Crystal the minute I saw her, but I had to play my cards right. We would have our meeting, and the whole truth would surely come out when we did.

Chapter 29

Mariah

Everything was absolutely beautiful as I looked around my home. The lights were low, red and white roses everywhere, and a beautiful ice sculpture of our last name stood on the table, along with various pictures of Malcolm and me throughout the previous ten years. Although I'd gotten goosebumps at the sight of it all, I still wasn't feeling about the night how I thought I would. After I'd left Eva and the baby at the hospital a week ago, I wasn't sure of the fate of the night's events. Every time I called or texted, I never got a response, and even after I went to her home, knowing she was there, she still didn't answer. It wasn't until yesterday morning when I texted her that all bets were off and she would see no portion of the two hundred and fifty grand that she finally replied. Carrying on as if she'd held all the cards in her hand, she requested the money up front before going through with tonight, and she wanted nothing but cash. Luckily for me, I knew I could blame removing the money from our account on paying for tonight's festivities. I had to take it out bit by bit, but once I did, I'd taken it to her in agreement that she and the baby would be here tonight. I even scheduled a car to pick them up when I needed them.

Thinking of Eva and the baby, when I'd gone to drop off the money yesterday, she finally let me hold him. He was the cutest and most precious thing I'd ever seen, and as I looked at his little face, I saw nothing but Malcolm all through him. It was so unreal, and I didn't want to put him down. The only thing that made me hand him back to her was that after tonight, he'd belong to Malcolm and me, not her. After the night was over, my husband would know exactly how much I loved him. Just the fact that I'd gone through what I had for the past few months to prove another woman's child was his and being willing to share our lives with the child would prove everything.

Walking over to the huge glass patio windows, I watched the water hit the rocks, allowing my mind to travel back in time. Instantly, I began to feel a tear creep down my cheek as I thought about Moses, my younger brother. Even after all the time that had passed, I still couldn't believe he was gone. It all happened so fast, and there was no chance at all of saving him.

The day he passed was like any other typical Saturday in our family. My mother had taken us to the beach to play in the sun and sand and just be free like she'd often done. Everything was as perfect as could be. We were two young children just enjoying life to the fullest . . . at least that was until I heard my mother's last words, *"Mariah, honey, keep an eye on your brother. Mommy has to run to the restroom."* It was no big deal because we'd been to the beach a million times before, and I'd always watched Moses if she had to walk away. But that day, I was so focused on building my perfect little sand castle that I didn't notice when he'd gotten too close to the water.

Suddenly, I heard people around us start to scream. My mother came running toward us, calling his name repeatedly, and when I turned around, his little body had already been swept away by the water. My mother, the lifeguard, paramedics, and just about anyone who could or could not swim tried to go in after him, but it was much too late. When they discovered his body, he had already drowned. I remember my mother being extremely depressed afterward, so I thought she hated me. But after a while, my father made her realize she still had another child living that needed her. That's when he made us both vow never to talk about Moses' death again and try to move on the best we could.

I couldn't help but think of how much I was like my mother. I was willing to cover up my true feelings regarding Malcolm and his affair so that everyone would continue to think we were the perfect little couple. It was just like how my mother covered up her true feelings regarding me and the entire incident so everyone would continue to think we were the perfect family. She took her real feelings with her to her grave, and I didn't find out until she was gone and read the journal she'd kept. That was why I'd started my journal six months ago when I found out about Eva, so if anything happened to me before it did Malcolm, he would come to know exactly how I felt. But before that time came, I decided to remain quiet.

"Baby?" Malcolm entered the room and snapped me out of my thoughts. "Everything looks amazing. I can't believe you and Crystal put all this together by your-selves."

"You really like it?" I asked, trying to wipe away any trace of tears before turning to face him.

"I love it, baby. But what's wrong?" He looked at me. "You look like you've been crying."

"I just can't believe we've made it this far, Malcolm. Marriages no longer last until 'death do us part' the way they used to, and these past few months have truly been our testament of *for better or for worse*."

"I know, right?" He walked closer to me and put his arms around me. "But we vowed till death do us part, Mariah, and I meant that with everything inside of me. I may have made my share of mistakes, but as long as you're willing to have me, I will make it all up to you."

"You promise? I mean, even if I can never give you a child from my womb? You still want to be with me?"

"I promise, Mariah Carter. It's me and you until the end of time."

I laid my head on his chest as the words came from his lips, and for the first time in months, I allowed myself to feel some sense of comfort with my husband. However, little did he know it would be me, him, Eva, and Malcolm Junior until the end of time.

We stood there, holding each other in the privacy of our home, when we heard the doorbell ring and knew our guests had begun to arrive. Whether or not either of us was ready, the night was about to start, and before it was all over, Malcolm's and my lives would be changed from that point forward.

"Happy anniversary, Malcolm Carter," I whispered in his ear. "I love you."

"Happy anniversary, sweetheart. I love you more."

Anthony and Angie were the first ones to arrive; then maybe ten minutes later came Carl and Symone, and after them were finally Cedric and Crystal. The minute they arrived, I met Crystal at the door.

"Girl, what took you so long? I thought you and Cedric would get here before anyone."

"I'm sorry, Mariah. Cedric and I had a bit of a disagreement that we needed to discuss before getting here."

"Is everything all right with you two?"

"Not quite, but I'll be fine. Just point me in the nearest direction of a glass of champagne. I'm about to take full advantage of having a babysitter tonight."

She walked away from me, and I immediately saw Angie walking over. "Mariah, I haven't been in your home in ages . . . practically since you and Malcolm married. It's beautiful," she said.

"It sure is," Symone chimed in as she came up behind her. "Makes me want to move right in." We all laughed together until Angie asked the fatal question.

"So, when will you and Malcolm start filling this huge house with the pitter-patter of baby feet? Isn't that why you all purchased such a lavish home?"

"We hope to soon, Angie," was all I could get out before politely dismissing myself and going over to the server with glasses of champagne. As I stood there trying to drown my cares in the golden tonic inside a flute glass, Anthony popped up in front of me.

"Mariah, have I told you how gorgeous you are tonight? Absolutely radiant," he said. I expected that from him. Anthony had the biggest crush on me in college and always swore he would make me his wife one day. Well, at least that was, until I met Malcolm and he met Angie. And although the two of us made the perfect match with two other people, it didn't stop his teasing and flirting.

"Well, thank you, Anthony. I truly appreciate that."

"And her husband does too," Malcolm said, walking up to us. I was positive he knew he had nothing to worry about regarding Anthony and me, but knowing my husband, that wouldn't stop him from marking his territory. So, the three of us stood there laughing and talking and catching up on life, love, and everything in between. That was, until I heard the doorbell ring and saw several of Malcolm's relatives walk in. It was the first genuine smile I'd seen come across his face when he saw his male cousins that I'd invited without his knowing.

"Michael, Hosea! Man, I haven't seen you guys in years," he exclaimed, walking over and giving hugs and daps.

They started having their man talk and catching up when the doorbell rang yet again. This time, I had no idea who it could be because many of our friends and family had already arrived . . . until the door opened and I saw her standing there.

"Miriam? Oh my God, Miriam, is that you?" I asked my stepsister, who I hadn't seen since we were children. I couldn't even find her to invite her to Malcolm's and my wedding. "What are you doing here? How did you know?"

"You aren't the only one with surprises," Malcolm said, coming over, grinning from ear to ear as if he'd pulled off the surprise of the century. "Happy anniversary, baby."

Miriam and I hugged, and I didn't want to let her go. She looked so much like our father that it was crazy, and I was sincerely happy for the first time in a very long time. Finally, I had many people I loved in one room. There was only one more thing that was going to make it complete. I watched everyone having the best time with one another, including Malcolm, and my heart was overjoyed. I couldn't wait to add the icing on the cake.

I looked at the display on my cell phone. It was almost nine, when I'd scheduled the car to pick up Eva and the baby. After that, they would be here shortly, and there would be no turning back. I was standing there, thinking about exactly what I planned to say, when Crystal approached me.

"This is a great anniversary party, girl, and believe it or not, your husband and I haven't had to kill each with our words."

"Look, I asked him to be on his best behavior, and that goes for you too, all right?"

"Okay, okay." She stopped one of the servers and grabbed a couple of hors d'oeuvre from his tray. "Anyway, when will we all find out about this surprise of yours? You know you have me on pins and needles."

"Soon enough, my dear friend. Soon enough."

Just as she kept trying to gather more information about the surprise, Cedric walked over and saved me.

"Happy anniversary, Mrs. Carter! This is a great party. I guess you've set the bar for Crystal's and my twentieth."

"Uh, I had a hand in planning this party too." She turned and playfully hit him on the shoulder.

"Well, as long as both of you plan ours just the same, I'll be happy."

We joked around a bit more before I realized I'd had a text from Eva saying they would be pulling up in about ten more minutes.

"All right, you two, I finally think it's time."

"Time for what?" Cedric questioned like a little kid.

"The surprise," I heard Crystal say quietly as her voice squeaked.

Then I took a spoon and began tapping the side of my champagne flute to grab everyone's attention.

"Attention, everyone, attention. Uh, if I could have my husband come and stand up here next to me, please."

Malcolm slowly moved in my direction. The room was so quiet that you could practically hear a pin drop. Once he made it to my side, I began to talk again, trying my best not to tear up.

"First, thank you all for being here tonight and celebrating Malcolm and me for our ten years of love, happiness, and pure wedded bliss. Now, don't get me wrong. As you all know, being married to this man has its challenges and ups and downs, but nothing that we couldn't face together and no challenges that I would have wanted to share with anyone else besides him. With that said, I wanted this night to be a night we would all remember. I wanted to surprise my husband with the gift of all gifts. I wanted to be able to tell my husband that we were expecting and going to start our family together," I said, looking around as the women in the room began dabbing their eyes with paper napkins and the men pretending as if they didn't want to cry.

I continued, "But as we all know, life doesn't always play out how we hope, expect, or plan. Uh, months ago, I found out that I may never be able to carry a child on my own," I said, hearing gasps throughout the room and feeling Malcolm grab hold of my hand with his that wasn't holding his champagne.

"Anyway, I said all of that to say that with encouragement from my doctor and the love from my husband, I found and believe that miracles can happen." I let go of Malcolm's hand, walked over to the door, and opened it to find Eva and Malcolm Junior standing there.

"Everyone, please, I would like to introduce you all to Malcolm Isaiah Carter II and his surrogate mother, Ms. Eva Tucker. Without her, none of this would be possible." I took little Malcolm from her arms and walked over to my husband. "Baby, meet your son, little Malcolm."

Malcolm looked at me with shock and confusion behind his eyes as his wineglass hit the floor. Then all at once, I started to hear the chatter of everyone in the room, questioning this and that and how this had happened. Then, before I knew it, Eva walked up behind me.

"Wait! This wasn't what we discussed. What do you mean by your 'surrogate'?"

"This isn't the time or place," I said to her softly.

"What is going on, Mariah? Is this supposed to be some practical joke?" Malcolm asked quickly, not seeming happy or enthused.

"Honey, no. This is your baby . . . our baby."

"Girl, wait. You already know about this woman?" Crystal asked out of nowhere. "Because I was just waiting for the right time to tell you."

"Tell her what?" Eva shot at Crystal.

"Don't involve yourself in this, Crystal. Please, leave it alone," Cedric told her.

The whole scene was complete chaos until Malcolm addressed our guests.

"Look, I'm sorry, everyone, but the party is over. My wife and I clearly have some things we need to hash out. And I'm sorry it had to end like this, but please, if you can all let yourselves out, that would be great. Thank you all for coming." He walked toward his study as I began apologizing to our friends and family before they left. That's when Eva reached for little Malcolm.

"Please, let me have my baby. You never said a thing about you and Malcolm keeping him and announcing me as just his surrogate. Whether or not you want to face it, *I* am his mother and *always* will be—*not* you."

"Mariah, do you want me to handle things here while you go and talk to Malcolm?" Crystal asked as if she were ready to fight Eva.

"No, no, everything is fine. You can go ahead and leave. Malcolm, Eva, and I will sort everything out here."

"Are you sure? Because—"

"Baby, say good night, and let's go," Cedric said, grabbing her arm and leading her toward the door.

A few minutes later, everyone except for Eva and the baby had left when I called Malcolm into the room. "Have a seat, Eva. Malcolm, can you come in here, please?"

"What, Mariah?" He stormed back into the room. "And what is *she* still doing here? Haven't you embarrassed me enough tonight?"

"*Embarrassed* you?" Eva called out. "How about I just gave birth to your son a week ago, and you haven't at least looked at him, held him, or anything? And on top of that, your wife passes me off as the surrogate. I'm sorry, but two hundred and fifty thousand just isn't worth all this."

"Two hundred and fifty thousand? Have you lost your damn mind, Mariah?" he yelled at me with his head looking as if smoke were coming from it.

"Why would you say anything about that? That was *our* agreement."

"Well, I'm sorry. The agreement is off," she said.

"And what agreement is this anyway? The 'Make Malcolm look like a complete fool for having an affair' agreement?"

"Stop it, stop it, stop it, stop it, please," I yelled at the top of my lungs, and suddenly, the baby began to cry. "Now, I'm sorry, everybody. This wasn't supposed to turn out this way. I honestly thought that I was doing something good—"

"Something *good?*" He cut me off. "You couldn't have thought that . . . not with all the sneaking and conniving that you've been doing for the past few months, not to mention trying to pay her off. Please tell me how that's something good, Mariah."

"If you would just calm down, I'll tell you. Now, first of all, I'm not the one who had an affair and got pregnant. That was all *your* doing, Malcolm, so if you want to point the finger and blame someone, blame yourself. I did this thinking that I could help Eva financially and also because you would have the opportunity to be in your son's life. I thought we could all come together for the sake of the baby. Nothing more, nothing less.

"Malcolm, I know I can never give you a child. We've been trying for the past six months, and longer than that, to tell the truth, and *still* nothing. And despite how much you say it doesn't matter to you, I know it does. So,

I thought I could give you what I knew you truly wanted, even if it didn't come from me."

"And where would Eva stand in all of this, Mariah? Did you actually expect her to hand her child over to us?"

"If you did, that's certainly not what *I* agreed to. I would never give my child to anyone else to raise, no matter how much money they offered," Eva chimed in.

"Listen, first, I think you should start reading things in full that you sign instead of simply looking at the dollar figures," I shot toward Eva. "And no, Malcolm, I didn't expect her to just hand her son over to us. On the contrary, I hoped she would do what was best for him by allowing him to be in a two-parent home while still being a part of his life. I thought it would be best for everyone involved."

"This is too much. I can't and won't deal with this tonight. I'm going for a drive. I'll be back later."

"Malcolm? Please, don't leave here like this. We'll work through all of this, but don't leave," I begged, grabbing his arm, but he snatched it away from me and kept walking toward the door. I wanted to go after him, but I knew it would be best to leave him to himself and give him time to cool down. With that said, I turned around and almost forgot about Eva and the baby still being there.

"Um, please allow me to apologize to you. I guess I've made a huge mess of things, so I'm sorry. You and the baby are welcome to stay the night in one of our guest rooms since it's so late, or I can call and have a car take you back home. It's up to you, but honestly, I would really like it if you stayed."

"I don't know. I'm sure Malcolm will come back, and I don't know if it will be good if I'm still here."

"Eva, please, stay. I'm not positive my husband will return, and I don't want to be here alone tonight. Please."

She didn't put up a fight, so I showed her to one of the guest suites for her and the baby to get comfortable in. Ironically, I'd bought all kinds of things for the baby that I'd hidden away in that room because it was a room Malcolm never went in. After ensuring they were both comfortable and settled in, I went straight to the bedroom to get undressed. First, however, I looked at my cell phone to make sure Malcolm hadn't texted me. There was a text from everyone else *but* him. Of course, Crystal texted, wanting to know what was going on. My stepsister, Miriam, texted, asking to know if I was okay. And even Anthony had texted, offering his ear if I needed someone to talk to. But nothing from my husband.

Then, throwing my cell phone on the bed, I slipped out of my little black dress, turned on the shower, and crawled under the water, allowing it to consume me. All I wanted was to wash away my tears, pain, and memories from what was supposed to be the most unforgettable night in my life.

Chapter 30

Crystal

"Wow, and you said your friend knew nothing about that woman. You said I had to be insane for thinking like I did when he's been dealing with her all along and even has a child with the woman. I *knew* I was right all along," I gloated on the car ride home.

"Give it rest, all right, Crystal? There must be some reasonable explanation for all of this. Mariah said she used her as a surrogate so the baby *could* be Malcolm and Mariah's, and she just carried it."

"Are you *serious* right now, Cedric? You tell me why on earth they would use Eva Tucker from our high school as a surrogate when millions of other women could have done it for them. You refuse to believe anything negative about that man, right? What is it? Does he have something over *you* that I'm not aware of?"

"Crystal, I talked to him right before the party. I told him your suspicions of him and Eva, and he assured me that he had nothing to do with the woman, and I believe my friend, all right?"

"Well, I'm not sure why. There's probably a lot he hasn't shared with you," I let slip out from being furious that my husband was so gullible.

"A lot like what? What are you talking about, Crystal?"

"Nothing. Just forget I even said anything because the real point is that my best friend felt like she had to go to the lengths she did just to make him happy and keep her marriage intact, and I blame him."

"You were going to blame him regardless of whether he'd done anything wrong. So what is it with you when it comes to him? What's the *real* reason you hate Malcolm so much? Because it has to be something more than he made me late to some birthday party years ago."

"You wanna know the real reason, Cedric? It's because the man has my husband so wrapped around his finger that you might as well be fucking him instead of me. How about *that?*"

The next thing I knew, he pulled the car over to the side of the road, hopped out, and slammed the door shut.

"You know what? Here, you drive home. I'll walk the rest of the way because clearly, you care more about what happens in your best friend's home than your own."

"Stop being silly, Cedric, and get back in the car," I yelled, but he continued to walk away from me. "Cedric. Cedric!" I called some more until I gave up, crawled into the driver's seat, and sped off, passing right beside him.

I was furious with my husband and even more with Malcolm Carter. Had it not been for him turning me down all those years ago, I would never have gotten with Cedric in the first place. I never would have married him or had to pretend that he was the man I was truly in love with. Now, all I wanted to do was get home and love on my baby, the one thing that reminded me *nothing* of Cedric.

Thinking about CJ made me consider finally telling Cedric the truth—that lately, I'd been thinking about us separating or even getting a divorce. I was unsure if it was what I wanted to do, but tonight's argument had almost sealed the deal for me. Not to mention that seeing that woman with Malcolm's child made me feel some type of way. I was jealous and didn't know how much longer I could hide it, although I knew that telling Cedric the truth about my feelings would mean I would need to be honest with Mariah too. That was one thing I wasn't ready for and the only reason I hadn't said anything all this time. Plus, if I did tell her, it wasn't like Malcolm would leave her, turn around, and be with me. It was all a mess that I wasn't sure how to get out of.

Suddenly, I remembered the night before he and Mariah got married. If only I had been able to get to Malcolm the way I planned, maybe there wouldn't have been a wedding. I went there solely on a mission. I had planned on getting Malcolm to myself and telling him the plain truth about how I felt about him. I needed him to know, and once he did, I was willing to let the chips fall where they may. But then I saw him with her . . . hugging and kissing her like he wanted her more than anything. The sight of them together upset me so much that it made me sick, and I just left. Then the next day, I had to play like the happy and supportive maid of honor in my best friend's wedding to the man I'd been in love with since childhood. A tear slowly crept down my cheek, with all the thoughts streaming through my mind. Malcolm, Cedric, Mariah, and Eva were all in my head, and I wasn't sure what to do about them.

Chapter 31

Eva

"*Surrogate?* Really, Mariah?" I said to myself. She had to be out of her mind if she thought that would fly with me. I have to admit that part of me felt so bad for Mariah. Here it was, her husband had practically cheated their entire marriage; he just had a baby with the same woman he had an affair with; she could not give birth to a child for him; and she'd gone through all that she had just to make him happy. I didn't know what I would have done had I been in her shoes. But to think I would hand my son over to her and Malcolm to raise was positively crazy.

Looking around at my surroundings while rocking little Malcolm to sleep, I wondered if I were just as crazy as she was. What was *I* doing? Here I was, had just given birth a week ago, made an agreement with the wife of the man I loved and my child's father, and now, was about to stay the night inside of their home. If all of that wasn't insane, then I didn't know what was. However, I didn't feel bad about any of it. I loved Malcolm, and I could tell by the look in his eyes when he saw me standing there holding MJ that he loved me too. He'd promised me this life for years, and I was determined to have it, even if it meant somehow getting rid of *her*.

Laying MJ down on the bed, I started to look around the bedroom. There was so much glass and crystal everywhere. It wasn't a home made at all for a baby. Then I saw a photo album on one of the nightstands. Flipping through it, I saw old pictures of Malcolm from when he was younger. That was the very young man that I remembered and had fallen in love with. Immediately, I began to reminisce over our time as high school classmates. I thought about how we first met, becoming each other's best friends and, later, lovers. Malcolm had been the only man I ever truly loved since being a little girl, and here I was, the mother of his firstborn child.

Flipping several more pages of photos, I started to see him, his best friend Cedric, and none other than Crystal herself. So much of me hated her. I hated her in school and even now as an adult. Everyone knew then how much she liked him, and I'd bet my last dollar that she still did. Just the look in her eyes when she saw me standing there made me want to keep my promise to her that day at her car. I wanted to make her life a living hell simply because I knew how she felt about Malcolm. And then, looking at her husband, I had a feeling that he was probably much too good for her, and she didn't deserve him.

The last few pages were random pictures that looked like they came from their wedding. Looking at them made me think about the night before at his bachelor party. I was furious that Malcolm was going through with marrying her. He had continually told me that he wouldn't do it, and if he did, it would only be for a little while. Finally, he said he needed to think of a way to get out of it. I didn't want him to go even that far.

I recalled calling his cell phone repeatedly, and when he didn't answer, I went to the hotel where he said they were. I told him that if he didn't come downstairs and talk to me outside, I would bust in and tell everyone about him and me. He knew I was dead serious, so he came down.

While his best man and groomsmen were getting pissy drunk and rubbing on the tits and asses of strippers, he was outside pleading his case with me. I begged him so much that night not to go through with it. I'd even suggested that we run off somewhere together without telling anyone. But he said he couldn't do it. He told me that if his parents, friends, or anyone found out we were together, he'd lose his inheritance and family fortune from his father. However, he assured me he would leave her. He promised that, eventually, he would divorce her, and it would be just him and me till death do us part. Then he kissed me, and I suppose that's when Crystal saw us. What I wasn't sure of was what she'd come there for—her husband or Malcolm.

After noticing little Malcolm wiggling, squirming, and whimpering, I knew exactly what time it was. He was hungry, and I was his bottle, so the pictures, thoughts, and plans all had to take a backseat so that I could give him my undivided attention.

I picked up my baby and prepared to feed him when I heard what sounded like someone coming in the front door. Trying to keep the baby quiet, I quickly put my nipple inside his mouth. I wanted to hear any interaction between Malcolm and Mariah that might occur. Then in pure silence, I listened to the strong footsteps moving around the front of the house. I was sure that if I heard him, Mariah had to also, so I waited to see if she would confront him.

The next thing I knew, someone's shadow stood outside the bedroom door. I was sure the person was simply walking past, but the shadow remained and never moved. My heart raced when the doorknob slowly turned. Then, there he stood, looking at me as I looked back at him, both of us in shock and confusion.

Chapter 32

Malcolm

Ever since I left, I'd driven around, trying to understand my wife and make sense of what she'd done. Of course, I knew that she desperately wanted to give me a child. I also knew that getting the news about needing a hysterectomy tore her up. But to involve my Eva and try to use her as a surrogate was nothing less than insane. I didn't know what to think or how I felt at that moment about her or the state of our marriage. True enough, I still loved her, but she'd shown a side of herself that I didn't even know was there and really didn't like. I wasn't sure how we were going to move forward, but one thing was for sure . . . It wasn't going to be without my son and his mother.

After walking into the house, I was glad that everything was quiet. It seemed that Mariah had already turned in for the night. There was no way I could have had any emotional conversation with her. Plus, I was positive that anything I had to say would have come out entirely wrong anyway. So, with that in mind, instead of going to our bedroom and possibly finding her awake, I went into the kitchen and poured myself a strong drink.

As I leaned against the island and downed the healing tonic, I could only think about Eva and the baby. I wondered about the day he was born, when he'd come into the world, and how I'd missed out on the first few moments of his life.

Immediately, I felt myself becoming infuriated. Yet, I wasn't sure if I was more upset with myself or Mariah. True enough, I hadn't even believed Eva when she first announced that she was pregnant. But now that he was here, all I wanted was a relationship with him—by any means necessary. However, a part of me feared that Mariah had messed up any chance of that happening with the stunt she'd pulled tonight. Eva more than likely thought the woman was crazy and didn't want our son anywhere around her. It was a mess, and I had to find a way to fix it, if for nothing else, then especially for little Malcolm's sake.

I thought of him, and a lonely tear fell from my eye. I longed to hold my one and only son for the first time. I wanted to look into his little eyes and assure him that I'd always be there, and that's what I planned to do the minute I contacted Eva. I wanted to make sure she knew that despite my marriage, I would assume my responsibility and always care for my son and her too, for that matter.

Continuing to think this whole situation through, I took one more shot, turned off the kitchen light, and headed to one of the guest bedrooms. Although my entire home was beautiful, I rarely went inside any guest bedrooms for anything. I usually only walked right past them and settled for either the master suite, my study, the theater room, or my man cave. But tonight, one of the guest rooms would be my home until Mariah and I figured out this mess.

Going to my room of choice, I found it odd, when I approached the door, that it was closed. It was never like Mariah to shut any of the doors in the house, so it struck me as a bit strange. Then I also noticed a small glimpse of light from underneath the crack at the bottom of the door. I couldn't help but wonder if maybe Mariah had the same idea as I did and she'd beat me to sleeping in the guest room. With that being the case, I turned around and decided to go to our bedroom and deal with things in the morning.

However, the alcohol I had in my system suddenly encouraged me to confront things head-on, and there was no time like the present. So, instead of heading to our bedroom, I decided to face the inevitable and have this much-needed discussion with her tonight. Opening the door, I could only stand there with a stunned look, and hers reflected the same.

"Eva?" I questioned, wondering what the hell she was doing there but also, at the same time, happy she was there. "What are you doing here?"

"Honestly, I don't know. After you left, your wife said she didn't want to be alone and asked if the baby and I would stay. It was already late, so here I am," she said innocently enough.

I walked into the room and closed the door behind me.

"Are you all right?" she asked.

"I don't know. I mean, I think so . . . or at least I will be. But the one question I've been curious about all night, Eva, is what made you go along with this whole charade that Mariah put on in the first place? I asked you to lie low until we had a paternity test done and I figured out how we should move forward. So how did you get mixed up with Mariah?"

"I guess I should be completely honest with you," she said as I watched her remove her breast from the baby's mouth, put him over her shoulder, and pat his back.

"Yes, please," I said.

"Well, all those months ago, you didn't even believe I was pregnant and threatened to walk out of my life completely. One night, I tried reaching out to you so that we could talk, but she answered your phone instead."

The minute she said Mariah had answered my phone, I lost track of the rest of her words, and my mind went back to the night I'd left my phone in the drawer in my study. It was then that I figured out why I found my phone face up. Instantly, it dawned on me that my wife had pretty much played me for a fool the entire time. She'd planned this whole scheme and left me clueless for months. Then all at once, my ears returned to what Eva was saying.

". . . but basically, it was the money, Malcolm. You didn't even believe I was pregnant and stopped communicating with me altogether. I had no idea how I would care for him alone, and your wife offered a way out as long as I helped her. She paid for the doctor's visits, baby items, clothes, and my entire delivery. And on top of that, she offered me two hundred and fifty grand if I went along with things. She even made me sign something consenting to everything. But, Malcolm, I never agreed to be anyone's surrogate. In fact, after she paid me the money, I planned to leave and never return."

When she mentioned leaving, I honestly felt some type of way about it. I couldn't imagine her and little Malcolm disappearing without me ever seeing them again.

"Eva, I admit I behaved foolishly when you told me you were pregnant. But now that we're here, and he's here, I don't know what I would have done if you and the baby left and I never saw either of you again."

"What exactly are you saying? I mean, where do we go from here?"

I'd heard her question, but instead of answering it, the next thing I knew, I reached in, and my lips connected with hers. Suddenly, a rush came over me, and I started to reminisce on all my years with her. My mind traveled down memory lane as I thought about her body, her giving me head, and me being inside of her. I wanted that again in the worst way possible, but I didn't know how I could with my wife in the next room. We must have been thinking the same thing because Eva suddenly pulled away from me just as we both allowed our tongues to glide in tune with each other's.

"Malcolm, wait. What are we doing? Your wife is right in the next room."

"Really? Is this coming from the same woman who came here butt naked under a trench coat and put me inside her mouth at my front door?"

"Okay, yeah, but that was a different time. I was a different person then. I wasn't someone's mother. Plus, I kind of understand and sympathize with your wife. She's going through a lot right now, Malcolm. I don't know what I would do if I were in her shoes and your mistress had your first child . . . something I could never give you. It probably would have driven me to do something crazy too."

"I hear you, but what she did tonight changes everything."

"Really?"

"Yes, it does. But honestly, I don't want to talk about Mariah anymore. I would much rather hold my son if you don't mind."

She looked shocked at my request but stopped mid-motion from patting his back and placed him in my arms. Instantly, it was like fatherhood had kicked right in. I held him and, looking down at him, automatically loved him with all my heart and wanted to protect him with everything inside me. Then, from out of nowhere, millions of thoughts rushed through my mind. I started to consider no longer being with my wife and being a part of Eva and Malcolm's lives. The only problem was going to be the fact that Mariah was sure to get more than half of everything that belonged to me. A judge would definitely award her practically whatever her heart desired because of my infidelity. With that in mind, my thought of being with Eva and the baby left just as quickly as it had come.

"Malcolm, are you okay?" she asked.

"I am, but I just really wish there was some way that you, the baby, and I could be a family without me losing everything I'd worked so hard for."

The room became silent until she said, "Maybe there is."

I looked into her eyes while asking myself what she'd possibly been contemplating. Whatever it was, I wouldn't agree to it unless there was a surefire way for me to keep my riches. Otherwise, I would be stuck in a marriage I no longer wanted to be in. Little Malcolm now meant more to me than anything or anyone . . . including Mariah.

Chapter 33

Mariah

I had heard Malcolm enter the front door over an hour ago, but it wasn't until a few seconds ago that I felt him crawl into bed next to me. I thought maybe he'd been in his study, his man cave, or even just laying on the couch in the living room as he sometimes did. But deep down in my heart, I knew that he'd more than likely found Eva in the guest room. I wanted to hold my peace, especially with all that had happened earlier, but something just wouldn't let me.

"Where have you been?" I asked after about ten minutes of him lying there with his back to mine. He didn't answer my question right away, so I asked again. "Malcolm, I know you're not asleep, and I know you heard me. So where have you been?"

"Mariah, please, not tonight, all right?"

"If not tonight, then when? You know we have to discuss this."

"We will, but only when I'm good and ready. There's been way too much that's happened tonight, and I'm not in the mood to talk about anything. It's late, and I just want to get some rest."

"So, it's what *you're* in the mood for? Forget *my* feelings, Malcolm? You're not even going to try to understand why I did what I did?"

"Not tonight, I'm not. Mariah, you have snuck around, schemed, and lied for the past six months or so. Even when I told you we would work things out together, you still did what *you* wanted to do, and *now,* you want to explain your actions? No. I'm not hearing it until I'm good and ready."

"Malcolm, have you forgotten that this all started because *you* cheated on me, slept with her, and got her pregnant? Do you remember *that,* or is that not supposed to matter?"

"It matters, and I've acknowledged what I did was wrong and apologized a million times over. But that still never gave you the right to go behind my back and make some foolish deal with her to take her baby. I mean, two hundred and fifty thousand grand, Mariah? Is *that* what our marriage is worth to you? Is that all my *son* is worth? And let's not forget the fact that you lied earlier and said the money was for the party."

His words hurt me to the core since, after all this time of not accepting that she was pregnant, he now acknowledged his son.

"I just wanted to give you what I couldn't. I thought the baby would do better in a two-parent home, and I figured she needed financial help anyway, so that's why I did what I did."

"And you never thought once that she didn't *want* to hand over her baby like she never had him?"

"Look, I'm sorry, okay? I guess I didn't think things through. But, Malcolm, where do we go from here? You and I are still married. You now share a son with her. So, how are the three of us going to move forward?"

"You mean the four of us . . . and I don't know. But I can't think about this tonight, so I'm going to sleep in another room. We'll talk in the morning."

Without allowing me the chance to say anything else, he got up and left our room just as quickly as he'd come in. I wanted to run after him, but something inside told me to leave well enough alone.

As I lay there staring at the ceiling, suddenly, my mind went back to that day at the doctor's office when Dr. Taylor asked if I believed in God and miracles. Since that day, I'd thought about having a relationship with God, but honestly, I hadn't done much to cultivate one. Instead, my mind had been totally focused on Malcolm and trying to make *him* happy. So, here it was. I'd gone behind his back and practically blackmailed his mistress into signing over her child for money just to make him happy, while I still felt empty and incomplete about it all.

All I wanted was my husband and the marriage I'd had for the past ten years, but I didn't know if that was still possible. It wasn't until that very moment that I realized that I truly needed things to change, and for the first time in my life, I knew that God was the only one that could make that change.

With that in mind, I crawled out of bed and knelt beside it. Because I'd never been much of the praying type, I didn't know what to say or how to say it, so I simply spoke from my heart. I asked God to forgive me for what I'd done, to allow my husband to forgive me, and even Eva. Then I asked him to fix my marriage. I begged God to help me do whatever I needed to get things back on track. I even asked him to perform a miracle by allowing me to one day get pregnant with my own child. I sealed the deal by letting God know I fully trusted him in whatever direction he led me. Finally, I told him I loved him and thanked him for my life thus far.

Right after my prayer, however, was when I learned to be careful what you pray for because you just might get it. Only thing is, it might not come exactly the way you expect it to. So, beginning that night, my whole life changed right before my very eyes.

Chapter 34

Crystal

A month had passed since the last time I'd seen Mariah at her and Malcolm's ten-year anniversary party, and I was finally happy to get some girl time with my best friend. We'd texted or called occasionally, but our communication was so short that it was never anything to write home about. So now, I needed some much-needed girl time to find out what had been going on in her world and to share what had been happening in mine.

Once I pulled up to their home, I was shocked to see a brand-new truck sitting in the driveway. Mariah hadn't said anything about her or Malcolm getting anything new, so I couldn't wait to hear who it belonged to. Going to the door, I rang the bell a couple of times before she finally answered.

"Hey, girl, I'm sorry. I was in the back bedroom."

"Oh, that's okay," I said, going right in and following her to the kitchen. "I wasn't out there long. But, uh, speaking of outside, I saw something really pretty sitting in the driveway. Who's got the new wheels?" I asked, sitting down at the island.

"You really wouldn't believe me if I told you," she said, grabbing a huge bowl of salad she'd prepared from the refrigerator. "It's actually neither of ours," she said hesitantly. "It belongs to Eva."

"Wait, that's a brand-new 2023. I wasn't aware she had money like that."

"Honestly, she doesn't," Mariah finished while setting two bowls down, one in front of me and the other in front of her. "Malcolm got it for her. He felt she needed something newer than what she had to take the baby to doctor's appointments and different things. Nothing is too good for his son and his son's mother." It came out very sarcastically.

"Now, Mariah, do I detect some jealousy?"

"Crystal, I wouldn't say that I'm jealous or anything. Maybe I was when I first learned about her, but not anymore. It's just that ever since the baby came into our lives, I don't feel like I know my husband anymore. He's been running around here buying her this and buying her that, all for the baby's sake, while she's been freely taking everything he's given. And in the meantime, I've felt like we've been growing further apart, and I'm on the outside looking in at *their* relationship."

"Wow, I had no idea. Have you talked to him at all?"

"Girl, I've tried . . . several times. But he always tells me everything is all in my head, and I'm just making up things. He claims that all he's doing is trying to be a good father to his son and that I have nothing to worry about, but I don't know, Crystal. Something just doesn't feel right anymore."

"I guess I'm curious to know how you guys even got this far. The last time we truly spoke was the night of the anniversary party."

"I know, and I'm sorry for being so distant, but I've been trying to handle things as best I could."

"So, what happened that night?"

"Not much, honestly. He left here all upset, and I didn't want to be here alone, so I asked her to stay, and she slept in one of the guest rooms. Then when he did return, he didn't have much to say to me and slept in one of the guest rooms himself."

"I see," I said as we both nibbled on our salads silently until I simply had to ask. "Girl, look, I just have to know. Did you *really* think she was going to hand over her child to you and Malcolm to raise?"

"Crystal, honestly, I wasn't thinking about anything but making my husband happy and giving him the child I knew he wanted. I mean, you should see him and the way he dotes all over little Malcolm. Plus, I figured the money I offered her would give her an edge in life. Something it didn't seem like she had."

"I guess I hear you, Mariah, but it was still a crazy idea if you ask me. Besides, why are you going out of your way to make him happy when he's clearly not making you happy? And him and his little mistress running around here as if they're some happy couple? Girl, please. I say divorce him and take him for every single penny he has. You already know that once a judge hears about his infidelity and that he got another woman pregnant, she'd be completely on your side. You can remain living the life you have become accustomed to and let them be broke and together."

"Yeah, I hear you, and trust me, I've thought about it several times, but then I go right back to the baby and what that would mean for him. He's an innocent child who deserves the best life possible. He didn't ask to be born into this mess."

"Girl, I applaud and respect you for considering the baby, but that's their love child, *not* yours. So let *them* figure out how to care for him."

Things once again became quiet as I assumed she was trying to let everything I'd said sink in . . . until she snapped out of her haze.

"Well, enough about me. What's been going on with you?"

"Me? Oh, nothing much, I guess. Only that I've been speaking with an attorney. I think I want to get a divorce from Cedric."

"What?" she yelled at the top of her lungs. "Divorce? Why? What do you mean? You can't."

"Mariah, I can, and I am. Girl, I'm just not happy, and I haven't been for quite a long time. I think it will be for the best."

"But Cedric is such a wonderful man . . . nothing like that husband of mine."

"Listen, I never said he wasn't a wonderful man. But he's just not the man for me. To be totally truthful, I'm just not the woman he needs. I never have been and never will be."

"Oh, Crystal, why would you feel that way? And what does Cedric have to say about this? And what about CJ?"

"Well, we've only talked about it once, and he feels like whatever is going on with us, it's nothing that counseling can't fix. And as far as CJ, I won't keep him away from his son. He can still spend as much time as he wants with him. But this is about me and being happy. Completely happy, and, unfortunately, that's not with Cedric."

"Girl, you say that as if there's someone else. *Is* there another man?"

I heard her question but didn't know how to answer. There was no way on earth that I could look into my very best friend's eyes and tell her that I was in love with her good-for-nothing husband—or even the worst part of it all.

"No, there's no one else, Mariah. This is strictly about me and my happiness."

"Crystal, I never would have imagined you would feel this way. I thought you and Cedric would always be together . . . I guess the same way I figured Malcolm and I would always be together, and now look at us. I definitely wouldn't have ever imagined that we'd both be going through something in our marriages at the same time."

"Yeah, tell me about it."

As we finished eating, we talked a bit more about our husbands, relationships, Eva, and her son. Then suddenly, Eva and Malcolm came strolling in with little Malcolm like they were one big, happy family.

"Well, hello, Crystal. Long time no see." Malcolm attempted to welcome me as pleasantly as he could while going over and kissing Mariah on the cheek.

"Hello, Malcolm," I responded as dryly as I could, hating the sight of him with her and her child. Instead of Eva and I speaking, we just stared each other down with dirty looks.

"Baby, look what I bought for the baby," Malcolm said, setting a massive bag that was filled to the top in Mariah's lap.

"Malcolm, don't you think the baby has more than enough clothes?" She almost couldn't seem to mask the sound of disappointment in her voice.

"Honey, he's a growing boy. He can't have too much clothing."

"And I tried to stop him, Mariah, but you know how this father is when it comes to his son," Eva chimed in out of nowhere, having the audacity to rub his back in front of us when she spoke. It was all sickening, and my heart practically broke into pieces for my friend.

"They're nice," was all that Mariah could force herself to say about the items. "Crystal, why don't we go into another room and finish talking."

"Uh, actually, I think I'm going to head home. Cedric and the baby are out of town with his parents until tomorrow, and I want to take advantage of the peace and quiet," I said, focusing on Malcolm and Eva. Mariah ignored their cooing with the baby and walked me to the door. I turned to her before leaving.

"Mariah, you're more than welcome to come to my house for a little while if you just want to get away."

"Thanks, but I think I'm going to stay here. Besides, she'll be leaving soon anyway."

"All right, girl, you're a much better woman than I am. But listen, you should really think about what I said earlier. I can give you the number of my divorce attorney if you change your mind and need it."

"Okay, I'll think about it, but I know it won't be as easy for me as for you. Malcolm is an attorney, and I'm sure he'll have some tricks up his sleeve."

"I told you already, attorney or not, with you holding that infidelity card in your hand, you've already won."

We hugged, and as I left, I thought about how I meant exactly what I'd said. She was a much better woman than I could ever be in that situation.

Chapter 35

Eva

"Uh, Malcolm, I think I'm going to head home too," I said right after Crystal left.

"Really? Why so soon?" He seemed extremely disappointed.

"I'm just kind of beat, and I'm sure MJ is all played out too, so I think we better get home."

"Well, I hope you and little Malcolm enjoy your evening," Mariah said with a smile as she returned to the kitchen. As much as she tried to hide it, I could see the enthusiasm written all over her face.

"Wait, why don't you let MJ stay over with Mariah and me? That way, you can get as much rest as you want, and he can get used to staying alone with me."

Once again, I looked at Mariah. Her face said it all. She didn't want MJ here with them any more than I did, so I tried to let Malcolm down as easily as possible.

"Honestly, I don't think he's ready for that just yet. Or at least, *I'm* not anyway."

"All right, well, I have to go out for something anyway, so I'll help you get MJ and his things inside the car."

He took MJ out of my arms, and they left the kitchen, leaving Mariah and me to our lonesome. Neither of us said anything at first until I decided to break the silence.

"Mariah, I'm sure this must be hard for you, so I just wanted to say how much I appreciate and respect your handling of everything. It's made this much smoother than I ever thought, so I just want to say thank you."

"Thank you for saying that, but there's no need at all to thank me. Little Malcolm is my husband's son, and we are going to do everything we can to make him know that he has a village of people that love him and give him the best life possible."

"Well, I wasn't talking about MJ as much as I was about myself. You didn't have to invite me into you all's life, and I'm just grateful for that. I wanted you to know."

"Eva, you are little Malcolm's mother, so that's all that matters."

Instead of pressing the issue any further with her, I decided to leave well enough alone. Then, a second later, Malcolm came back, inquiring if I was ready to go. So we packed the baby and his things in the car, and I pulled off as quickly as possible.

The entire way home, I kept thinking of how quickly I could get rid of Malcolm because I had something much more critical to take care of. I was tired of playing nice with everyone attached to this situation. It was time I got my point across. Immediately before I arrived at home, I made a call.

My neighbor answered on the first ring. "Hello?"

"Hi, Jasmine, it's Eva. I wanted to know if you were possibly free this evening and if you could come over and babysit MJ for an hour or so?"

"Um, yes, I'm free. I would love to watch MJ for you."

"Okay, great. Why don't you come over in an hour?"

"Sure thing."

Jasmine was the teenage neighbor who would come over occasionally whenever I needed to make a quick run. I'd lived next door to her and her parents for seven years. Outside of Malcolm, she was the only other person I trusted around my son. So, I was thankful I could count on her while I took care of things tonight. Then, finally pulling up in the driveway, I got out and started to remove MJ as Malcolm pulled up right behind me.

"So, do you think she suspected anything?"

"No, I think you played your role quite well. Too well, actually. You don't know how much it bothered me seeing you kiss her cheek and hearing you call her baby. I almost wanted to gag," I said, walking into the house. He followed right behind me.

"Yeah, I figured that was why you suddenly wanted to leave. But we both agreed that I needed to continue playing the loving husband until we figure out how to be together."

"I know, Malcolm, but I don't know how much longer I can do this. I'm tired of being overly nice to your wife, and seeing that friend of hers pissed me off more than you know."

"Who? Crystal? She should be the *least* of your worries."

"She is, but I just hated the way she kept looking at me with that ugly, stank expression all over her face. I just wanted to smack it off her," I said, going to lay MJ in his crib since he was fast asleep. Then, as I came back into the living room, I saw that he'd removed his shirt and pants.

"Malcolm Carter, what are you doing?"

"Look, I've been going crazy all day to be inside of you. Come and make my wish come true, my beautiful Eva."

I walked toward him, sat him on the sofa, and straddled my legs around him. "I don't want to be with you again, only for you to run right back to her and lie beside her and who knows what else you do with her when I'm not there."

"Listen, you don't have to worry your little head about that. I've been disconnected from Mariah in every way possible for the past month, so you have nothing at all to be concerned with. I am all yours . . . and MJ's too."

We both laughed as I crawled off his lap and onto my knees, immediately putting him inside my mouth. I wanted to give him exactly what I knew he'd been missing and what I'd longed for too. However, I kept in the back of my mind that I needed to get rid of him as quickly as possible. Tonight would be the only night I could do what I needed to do, and nothing on earth would stop me. Not even getting fucked by Malcolm.

An hour later, he came out of the shower and began drying off and getting dressed.

"Are you sure you don't want me to stay the night with you and MJ?"

"Really, Malcolm? So that wife of yours can be over there going crazy? No, thank you. Besides, I have something I need to take care of," I said, hearing Jasmine ring the doorbell.

"Who's that? And what do you have to do?"

"That's my neighbor who will watch MJ while I step out for a second." I opened the door and greeted her with a hug. All at once, I could see the look in Malcolm's eyes as if he knew I was up to something. Then, out of nowhere, he grabbed my arm and pulled me aside.

"What's going on, Eva? Where are you headed that you can't tell me, and if you needed someone to stay with MJ, then I could have done that," he said softly so Jasmine couldn't hear.

"No, you couldn't have because you have a wife to get home to. And I have something I should have taken care of a while ago. I can't tell you now, but you'll find out soon enough. I told you I would handle everything from here on out."

"I don't know what that means, and I must be honest. That's what's scaring me the most."

"Please, just trust me and know that everything I do, I do for you."

I gave Jasmine some instructions, grabbed my keys, and headed out the door with Malcolm. After he got inside his car and left, I drove off toward my destination. The whole way there, I kept asking myself if this was what I wanted to do, but I felt it was too late to back out. What I was about to do needed to be done, and it had to happen tonight.

Chapter 36

Crystal

I was glad I left Mariah's when I did. Seeing Malcolm all googly-eyed with that woman's child was tearing me up inside, and had I stayed any longer, I knew I would have reacted outside of myself. Plus, I was positive my thoughts and feelings were written all over my face regarding Eva. I didn't care for her way back in the day, and the feeling was still the same. I didn't like how she was throwing her relationship with Malcolm in Mariah's face. And no matter what they'd tried to make Mariah believe, my gut told me way more was going on with them than they were letting on.

Once I arrived home, I looked around and thought about how happy and at peace I was alone without Cedric. Of course, I missed my baby boy like crazy, but the night alone and all to myself was very much needed. It gave me time to think through and consider all my options before making a drastic decision.

Still a little hungry after the salad at Mariah's, I cooked some salmon in the oven. Then I poured a glass of red wine, turned up some jazz, and lit candles throughout my home. I also took out my journal to do some writing while I ate. Journaling had become a favorite pastime of mine. It allowed me to release all the secrets I'd held inside of me and look back on my life and see how far I'd come.

I sat down and grooved to the smooth tunes while I ate, drank several glasses of wine, and wrote my thoughts without inhibitions. I wrote about speaking with a counselor and attorney about a divorce. I wrote about how happy and free I already felt at the mere thought of no longer being married to Cedric. I wrote about Malcolm, my feelings toward him as well as Mariah, Eva and her baby, and even my CJ. I let go of every little secret inside of me, and it was the most freeing feeling and the most relaxed I'd felt in quite a long time.

Then afterward, I ran a bubble bath to unwind and release even more. I put all types of scented oils and things inside the water and allowed them to dissolve. After that, I cut out the bathroom light and sank right in. It was practically like heaven on this side of earth, and it seemed like I drifted off to never-never land the second I got in.

The water was having its way with me as it took over every crevice of my body. Slowly, I allowed my mind to drift to Malcolm. I thought about that day he and Mariah came over to see CJ, when he put his hand inside my panties. I could feel his strength as he touched my clit, and I recalled how much I wanted to scream with passion. I desperately wanted that feeling again, so much so that I put my hand under the water and began touching myself. I moved to the sound of the music and the motion of the water as I slowly stimulated myself. It was how I longed to feel Malcolm touch me. I dreamed of him kissing me, sucking on my breasts, and licking between my thighs. All my visions overtook me, and before I knew it, I felt my ultimate release in sight.

As my body shook in pure pleasure, I called out Malcolm's name. Then suddenly, I heard a sound inside the living room. Trying not to panic, I figured that maybe Cedric and CJ had come home early, and he had bumped into something since all of the lights were out.

"Cedric? Cedric, is that you? What's wrong? You got tired of having CJ all to yourself, huh? Mommy's baby must have been fussy," I joked with him, but the weirdest thing was I didn't hear a response in return. Then, whoever was there turned up the music even louder. Next, I heard footsteps come closer toward the bathroom. Foolishly, I hadn't taken my cell phone in the bathroom with me, so I tried to think of the best way to get to it to call someone.

"Who's there?" I continued to call out, but there was still nothing . . . until I saw someone's frame standing in the dark.

"Who are you? What do you want? Please take anything in my home, but don't hurt me," I pleaded.

Before I knew it, the unknown person flicked on the light to reveal who it was.

"What the hell are you doing in my home?" I questioned. She was dressed in all black and even wore a ski mask and gloves.

"I tried to warn you before, Crystal, to stay the fuck out of Malcolm's and my business, but you just wouldn't listen, huh? You had to make your accusations, give your theories to Mariah, and how you had the nerve to look at me earlier like I was the scum of the earth. Who the hell do you think you are?"

"Eva, please. How did you get into my home? What are you doing here? And what do you want?"

"Don't you get it yet, Crystal? I'm here to keep the promise I made. I told you that if you kept it up, there would be hell to pay. Well, welcome to hell, bitch." She walked closer to me and grabbed my wet body.

"Eva, please," I screamed with everything I had inside me. "What are you doing? Please, don't hurt me."

"It's too late for all that," she said as we tussled. "I've hated you for so long. All I can remember is how you and your snooty-ass friends used to turn up your noses at me and act as if you were better than me. Well, who's in control now, little miss snooty? Who's got the upper hand now?"

"Eva, please, you and I both have so much to live for," I tried to beg her. "You have MJ, and I have CJ. Please, don't do this to either one of them."

"Bitch, keep my son's name out of your mouth," she said as she punched me in the face. Then she started hitting me elsewhere. I kept trying to scream, but nothing would come out. Finally, I assumed out of exhaustion, she stopped.

I felt like her rag doll and almost wanted to succumb to my injuries, but I couldn't. I had to fight back. Picking up my wineglass sitting on the tub, I took it and hit her over the head. It didn't have the effect that I thought it would, other than pissing her off even more.

"You stupid bitch," she yelled as we both began to struggle again, and the only leverage I had was that the water had my body so slippery it was difficult for her to grab hold of me.

"Eva, please, please, stop it. Please don't do this to my son."

"I don't give a damn about your kid. Did you care about *me* as a kid? He'll be better off without you anyway."

"Eva, you don't understand. My son is your son's brother. Please, don't do this to them."

All at once, she stopped and just stared at me. "What the hell do you mean, my son's brother?"

"Eva, my son is not my husband's child. He's Malcolm's. He and MJ are half-brothers."

"No, you're lying. That can't be. Malcolm would never be with a woman like you. And you're Mariah's best friend, for goodness' sake. What type of woman are you?"

"I don't know, Eva. I've been in love with Malcolm ever since we were children. Mariah doesn't know how I feel, and she and Malcolm have no idea about Cedric Junior. Neither does my husband. But I promise that if you don't hurt me, I'll come clean to everyone about everything. I promise."

Those were my last words before we fought some more. Finally, I could no longer match her strength. She began to push my head farther and farther underwater. . . until I couldn't feel anything anymore.

Chapter 37

Mariah

My eyes popped open, and my back shot up straight. As I felt around on the other side of my bed, my mind started to wander, and my heart raced in a panic when Malcolm's solid, muscular frame was nowhere to be found. Quickly, I slid my feet into my slippers while wrapping my black satin robe around my body.

"Malcolm? Malcolm?" I called out as I began to walk from room to room, looking for any signs of life. There was no response, and immediately, I felt a chill shoot straight through my body, leaving goosebumps down my arm. Something was odd, extremely odd, about the night, but for the life of me, I couldn't seem to put my finger on it. Not to mention the dream that I'd experienced had me frantic. I couldn't trace all the details of it, but the last thing I recalled was his body lying on the other side of our bed—bloody and lifeless.

As I continued to check the rooms in the house, I felt a cold dampness throughout it, and all I could hear was the loud roar from the waves tossing and crashing against the rocks outside. The sound reminded me of all those years ago when we first married. I was so in love with Malcolm. He was the man of my wildest dreams, and I thought we'd be together forever. And now, I couldn't believe the state of our marriage.

I thought back to earlier and what Crystal had said before she left. Maybe it was actually time to let go. After all, my happiness did mean much more than what I was going through with him.

As I reached our living room, my eyes caught a quick glimpse of the display on our sixty-four-inch flat-screen TV. It was at that moment that I realized why I felt so unsettled. Malcolm had never made it a habit to come home after midnight, and the display on the screen read ten minutes after one in the morning. Although I didn't want to assume the worst, my gut told me that either something was completely wrong or that his lateness had to do with *her*.

Ever since I'd brought that woman into our lives, it seemed as if Malcolm was changing into someone I didn't know, and I'd been regretting this whole ordeal. He'd been telling me it was all in my head, but something wasn't adding up about her or their relationship. I hadn't said much to Malcolm about it for fear of seeming inse-cure, but with her holding all the right cards in her hands, it was a no-brainer. Not to mention her beauty alone was enough to make any man go crazy.

What on earth did you do, Mariah? Why did you ever bring this woman into our lives? I asked myself, finally making it to our kitchen. Grabbing my wineglass I had used earlier in the evening from the sink, I rinsed it out and poured the remaining contents of the wine bottle in-side. Then, leaning up against our white marble-topped kitchen island, I contemplated things further.

All I wanted was to give you a son, Malcolm, and now, because of it, our marriage might be destroyed. All at once, I started thinking of my next move, whether to call *her* directly and tell her to put my husband on the phone or go to her home to catch both of them red-handed. Either way, he'd be shocked because it was unlike anything I'd ever done. But I felt it was needed to put my mind at ease.

Pulling out another bottle of wine, I attempted to fill myself with enough liquid courage to do the latter. However, my practical side advised against it. Instead, with my wineglass in hand, I walked back into the living room, where I'd left my cell phone on the coffee table.

"All right, Mariah, are you *really* going to do this?" I questioned my alter ego. Then before I knew it, I downed the last bit of wine . . . and dialed her number.

"Hello?" She answered on the first ring in a soft and muffled tone. It was strange because I knew exactly what I wanted to say before I called, but having her on the phone suddenly made my mind blank.

"Hello? Mariah?" She called my name, I'm sure from seeing my number on the display.

"Uh, yes, is Malcolm—"

Before I could finish, someone rang the doorbell several times in quick succession. Looking out the glass doors that led from our family room to the patio, I could see blue and red lights flashing from several cars.

What are the police doing here? I wondered, praying it had nothing to do with my uneasiness about my husband. "Uh, hold on for just a sec. I need to get this." I slowly cracked the door open, and the tall, stocky gentleman quickly showed his badge.

"I'm sorry to come to your home so late, ma'am, but are you the wife of Mr. Malcolm Carter?"

Opening the door farther, I almost hesitated to answer. "Uh, yes, Officer, yes, I am. But what is this about? Is something wrong?"

"Mrs. Carter, I am Detective Wilson, and this is Detective Murphy. I hate having to tell you this, but—"

"But what?" I cut him off while recalling my dream. "What's going on?"

"Ma'am, I'm sorry, but there's been an accident involving your husband, and he's . . ."

At that very moment, I honestly didn't hear another word he said. All I can remember is my cell phone dropping from my hand and hitting the floor as I fell into the detective's arms in agony.

Chapter 38

Mariah

"Please, don't tell me my husband is gone," I cried out. "He can't be. He was just here, alive and well and happy. This can't be. Please."

"Ma'am, I'm so sorry," I heard the more compassionate detective say as he grabbed hold of me and allowed me to sob on his shoulder for a moment.

But then, the *all-business* detective got right back down to the matter at hand. "Mrs. Carter, it appears that your husband was in a terrible car accident. Unfortunately, his body must have been ejected, and we could not locate it, but please be assured that we are still searching. However, I must ask, does your husband have anyone in his life who may have wanted to harm him?"

"Harm him? Uh, no, not that I'm aware of. Why on earth would you ask me something like that?"

"Well, it appears his truck may have been tampered with or possibly run off the road, and that's how the accident occurred."

"No, Detective, no, that just can't be. My husband didn't have enemies like that."

"All right, well, I do need to ask you, how were things between the two of you?"

"What? What does that have to do with anything?"

"Ma'am, trust me, it's just part of the process for us to complete our report. So, were things well in your marriage? Would you have had any reason at all to hurt him?"

"Wilson, look, maybe we should finish this later or at a better time than tonight. Let's allow Mrs. Carter to rest and have her come into the station tomorrow," the kinder detective said as he helped me sit on my couch.

"No, I want to answer him tonight. Now, did my marriage have its issues? Yes. We've been married for ten years, so what marriage wouldn't go through things after that long together? But did I want to hurt my husband or have him killed? Definitely not. Regardless of what we've been through, I would have never wanted to harm him. I love my husband dearly with all my heart."

Although I felt I'd just poured my heart out to the man, he kept right on with his line of questioning, completely unaffected.

"So, there's never been any cheating or infidelity in your marriage?"

"You know what? I'm not going to do this with you right now. You just told me my husband, the only man I've ever loved, is gone. I need to deal with *that* instead of your insensitive questions."

"Mrs. Carter, we're very sorry, okay? My partner doesn't mean to be insensitive at all. We're simply trying to get some answers for you, and maybe it just came out the wrong way. Why don't I stop by tomorrow myself and speak with you further?"

"Uh, sure, that's fine, I guess."

They left, and instantly, I realized I was in that huge house all alone, and Malcolm was never coming back. Although I had a million thoughts running through my mind, I knew that I needed to hurry and contact his parents and family. Looking for my cell phone, it dawned on me that I had dropped it after calling Eva. I knew there was no way that she would still be on the phone, but when I picked it up, I heard her whimpering.

"Hello?"

"Mariah, please, tell me it's not true. Please tell me I didn't hear what I think I heard."

"I'm sorry, Eva, but I can't. Malcolm was in a terrible accident, and he's gone."

"Oh my goodness. I don't believe this. What are we going to do? I can't take care of MJ on my own. What am I supposed to do now?" she questioned.

"Eva, listen, taking care of little Malcolm should be your *last* concern. I will help with him as much as possible. If he's Malcolm's son, his flesh and blood, I will be here for him now more than before."

"I don't know, Mariah. None of this seems right. Malcolm being in an accident and me and the baby having to depend on you . . . It's just not right."

"You're not depending on me, all right? MJ is a Carter and the only one left to carry on the Carter legacy. He will be very well taken care of. Now, I have to go and call Malcolm's parents and other relatives and tell them the news. I'll talk with you later."

"Mariah, do you mind if MJ and I come by tomorrow? It would make me feel closer to Malcolm."

"Uh, sure, that shouldn't be a problem."

"Okay, good, and thank you so much for everything. Bye."

"Bye."

We hung up, and although I didn't want to think anything negative, I couldn't get past the fact that she hadn't seemed too torn up about Malcolm's death. Instead, she was more concerned about how she would care for little Malcolm. I didn't have time to focus on her, though, because I had to call his family and friends. However, I decided to hold off on Cedric until tomorrow. They were like brothers, and I was positive he would take the news harder than anyone.

After contacting a few of his relatives, I sat down and thought about what the detective had asked, whether anyone was looking to harm him. Even though I tried not to let my mind go to the worst possible scenarios, I wondered if there may have been any other women he 'd had an affair with, or if Eva was the only one. If so, they had more than enough reason to want to do something to him. Yet, no matter which direction my mind was trying to go, I still loved my husband.

With that thought, I took his picture from the mantle, sat on the sofa, and cried my heart out for the rest of the night. I almost wanted to call Crystal, since I didn't want to be alone and she'd invited me to come over earlier. But I knew it was late, so I decided to tough it out by myself through my tears.

Chapter 39

Eva

After hanging up with Mariah, my hand shook as I immediately dialed Malcolm's cell phone number. We'd devised a plan for us to be a family, but it never included any car accident, and things weren't supposed to happen this soon anyway. So, it frightened me that his death might be true. I repeatedly called, but there was nothing. All I got was his voicemail.

Then I recalled that as I listened on the phone, the detective asked Mariah if anyone had any reasons to harm Malcolm. I knew in my heart that she had more than enough reason to do something to him, but I would never have imagined her to do it. But if she had, how on earth would I prove this to the authorities? And better yet, how would I do it without incriminating myself in his or Crystal's death? Knowing I had way more to lose than anyone involved in this mess, I decided to keep quiet and play my cards right. I felt that if I remained by Mariah's side as much as possible, I could somehow work my way into getting most of Malcolm's money for MJ. Of course, I hated what had happened to Malcolm more than anyone, but what everything boiled down to now was guaranteeing that my son and I had everything we needed to live the life I wanted.

My doorbell rang as I got into bed to prepare for my emotional performance. I figured it was likely Jasmine because she'd left something at my house. But as I peeked out to be sure, I didn't see anyone there. At least that was, until a second later when Malcolm came out of the bushes. He looked like he'd been run over by a car or beaten up by a mob as I hurried to get him inside.

"Malcolm, what the hell? You had me scared to death."

"I know, and I'm sorry, but have the police contacted you?" he questioned in a panic the second he stepped inside.

"No, at least not yet. They just left your house to inform Mariah of your death."

"How do you know that?"

"She called me right before the police showed up with the news. I believe she thought you were here."

"Did you hear anything else?"

"Sure did. They said they couldn't find your body but were still searching. They also asked if anyone wanted to hurt you, and one of them is going back tomorrow to talk to her."

"Talk to her about what?"

"Whether *she* had anything to do with your death."

"What? No, no, no." He started pacing around with his hands on his head. "I didn't want her to get blamed for anything. I just wanted a way out."

"Yeah, but this wasn't what we discussed, Malcolm. It wasn't supposed to happen like this. But why don't you look at it as a good thing? If they do blame her, there's no way she can keep any of your money."

"Yeah, because she would be sitting in a damn jail cell." He stopped walking and sat down on my sofa. "I just figured I could fake my death to be with you and MJ for good. I don't want her to be accused of killing me."

"All right, but what about your money? If you're deceased and not accused, baby, she's sure to get everything now. So, now what?"

"No, no, she's not. I forgot that I recently redid my will. So, besides her getting something from one of my insurance policies, I left everything else to MJ. . . . my entire estate. So, all you have to do is exactly what I tell you to do, and our little family should be home free."

"I don't know about this, Malcolm. How on earth will we cover up the fact that you're still alive?"

"Listen, the police will never find my body because there isn't one. Then, once we officially get the money from my estate, we can change our identities and move away. No one will find us."

"I hear you, but I just don't think we've thought this through all the way."

"Woman, I need you to stop being so negative right now. I just faked my death to be with you and MJ, so you need to go along with this. You're the main one that's been begging me to do whatever was necessary to be with you and the baby. So, now it's done, whether either of us likes it."

I heard everything he said, but I still had my doubts. Something about it all wasn't sitting right with me, but I didn't know exactly what that was. Plus, I was sure the minute the police discovered I was Malcolm's mistress who'd recently had his baby, they would come knocking on my door. Then, not only would I have to explain our relationship, but they might also find out about my hate toward Crystal and connect me to that too. We were in a real bind, and Malcolm didn't even realize it.

"Baby, I need something to eat. Faking my own death has me famished." He walked into the kitchen, and I followed right behind him.

"Malcolm, um, I need to tell you something."

"All right, what's that?" he asked nonchalantly, not really seeming as if he were paying any attention as he took out bread and lunch meat.

"Well, remember when I told you I had something to take care of earlier?"

"Yeah." He continued preparing his food and poured himself a large glass of juice.

"I, um, I went to see Crystal."

"Crystal? Why the hell would you do something like that?"

"Malcolm, I was tired of her and how she looked at me and thought she was better than me."

"What? Do you know how you sound right now? Just like a teenage girl in high school. Are you *really* that concerned with how someone looks at you and what they think of you?"

"Look, I don't sound childish, and yes, I was that concerned. So, she got exactly what she deserved."

He set down his glass of juice and stared at me in shock. "What does that mean, Eva? What do you mean, 'she got exactly what she deserved'?"

"I don't know what happened, Malcolm," I said, trying to cough up some tears to gain his sympathy. "I only went to talk with her and ask what her problem has always been with me. I promise that's all I went to do."

"What the hell happened, Eva?" His voice rose.

"First, would you please try to calm down? You're going to wake up MJ."

"Eva," he whispered, "start talking and tell me what the hell happened with you and Crystal."

"All right, okay. When I got there, she was in the bathtub. Everything was dark, and she had music playing. I turned up the music and blew out the candles. Then I went into the bathroom where she was. She saw me and immediately began to argue. She said things, and then

I said things, and we were both yelling at the top of our lungs. Then out of nowhere, she threw a wineglass at me and tried to get out of the tub. Malcolm, I grabbed her, but it was only to make her calm down. But then, we struggled, and before I knew it, I held her head down in the water. I was going to let her up, baby, but everything happened so fast. And then a second later . . . She was gone."

"Gone? What the fuck do you mean 'gone'?"

"Gone, Malcolm. I killed Crystal," I said, never telling him one word about her saying CJ was his son.

"Oh my goodness. Oh no. This can't be. Please tell me you didn't do this, Eva. Tell me there's a chance she's still alive."

"Baby, I wish there was, but I can't. I checked for her pulse before I ran out of there."

"I don't believe you. I don't believe this. You're standing here telling me this story like it's a movie you just watched, but Eva, you just killed someone I've known my entire life. She's my best friend's wife and my wife's best friend, for Christ's sake. How could you *do* this? She has a son who will grow up without his mother. Did you think about *that* at all? What is *wrong* with you? What type of person are you?"

"The same type, dammit, that has given her entire life to you," I yelled, sick of listening to him carry on about his precious Crystal. "You took my childhood, my womanhood—everything from me. I've never been able to be with anyone else or find anyone that would love me and only me because you wanted me all to yourself. You didn't want me with anyone else while you kept promising and promising that you would leave that wife of yours and marry me. But guess what? You suddenly broke things off, Malcolm Carter, and after all these years and all the energy I put into us, *I* was the only one left to deal with it. Well, I'm tired of dealing with it. I'm tired of waiting for you to choose me finally. I'm tired of being fake friends with your wife, and I was sick of that dirty, smug, I'm-better-than-you attitude of your wife's best friend, who, by the way, just happened to be in love with you. So that's why the hell I did what I did. I'm sick and damn tired," I yelled, picking up his glass of juice and throwing it against the wall.

He sat there stunned and looked at me as if I were crazy. Neither of us said anything, I figured because we just didn't know what to say. Then, out of nowhere, I heard MJ screaming from the other room.

"I gotta get the baby." I walked out, leaving him to clean up the mess.

Chapter 40

Mariah

I pretty much hadn't slept all night, and now it was ten in the morning, and someone was at the door ringing the bell like the police were chasing after them. I figured it was likely one of Malcolm's relatives, so I threw on my robe and slippers and rushed to answer as quickly as possible.

"All right, all right, I'm coming."

As I opened the door, Cedric rushed in, in a panic and frenzy. I assumed he must have found out about Malcolm.

"Hey, Cedric, you must have heard about Malcolm."

"Malcolm? What are you talking about? I'm here about Crystal, Mariah."

"Crystal? What's wrong with Crystal?"

"Mariah, it looks like there was some type of accident in the house . . . the bathtub . . . and she's, she's, she's—"

He couldn't finish his sentence. Tears streamed down his face as he walked around in circles.

"All right, all right, wait a minute, Cedric," I said while grabbing him. "Look at me and tell me exactly what you're trying to say."

"Mariah, my parents and I got to the house, and she was in the tub . . . Her head was under the water. She's gone, Mariah. My wife is gone!"

There was no way I could believe my ears. First, the police showed up and said that my husband had been in a car accident, and now Cedric was telling me about Crystal.

"Wait a minute, Cedric. Are you sure? Did you call the paramedics?"

"Mariah, I called hours ago, the minute I found her. They pronounced her dead at the scene. They said she'd been underwater for too long, and there was no way they could save her. She's gone, Mariah. Then they asked if we had somewhere to go while they investigated the scene. My parents took CJ to their home, and I just needed some air. So, I figured I would stop by here and talk to you and Malcolm. Mariah, I honestly don't know what I will do without my wife."

I stared at him, not knowing what to say and definitely not about to tell him about Malcolm.

"All right, just try to calm down, Cedric, and let me get you some water," I said, running into the kitchen, then returning to the living room with it.

"Here, take this and have a seat. Just try to relax."

"You know, the crazy part about it all, Mariah, is that the police think there may have been some foul play, and they were questioning me about our marriage and my whereabouts. I explained to them that, yeah, Crystal and I had our ups and downs, but I would never, ever hurt my wife. I loved her. I still love her, Mariah. I love her," he kept saying as I watched him cry like a baby. I put my arm around him, trying to console him and not break down entirely myself.

"Everything's going to be okay, Cedric. We're going to get through this, all right? Somehow, we're going to get through this."

"Where's Malcolm?" he looked up and asked through tears.

"Malcolm?"

"Yes, Mariah, Malcolm. Is he here?" He stared at me, trying to search my eyes for an answer.

Just as I was about to reply, the doorbell rang again. Quickly, I excused myself and ran to open the door. Looking out, I rolled my eyes the second I saw her face.

"Eva? What are you doing here so early?"

"I'm sorry, Mariah, but I couldn't sleep with everything happening. Plus, I figured you would be awake. I also thought you might want someone by your side whenever the detectives return."

"Detectives?" Cedric asked, coming from the living room into the foyer. "What is she talking about, Mariah? What's going on?" he questioned, overhearing her words.

"Cedric, why don't we talk about this later, all right? And, Eva,"—I turned to her—"maybe it's a bit too early to be here. I'm not sure what time the detective will come by, and I need to finish talking with my husband's friend alone, if that's all right with you."

"Oh, all right," she answered, seeming bothered by my response. "I guess I can just come back later when it's more convenient for you."

She opened the door to leave, but just as she cracked it open, Detective Murphy walked up to my doorstep.

"Detective Murphy, hello, good morning."

"Good morning, Mrs. Carter. Is this a bad time?" he asked, looking at my attire and seeing Eva and Cedric standing there.

"Um, no. Detective Carter, this is my husband's best and closest friend, Cedric, and this is . . . um, his son's mother, Eva."

He shook both of their hands as I invited him in, and we all walked into the living room.

"Please forgive me for not being fully dressed. I just got out of bed," I explained until Cedric jumped in.

"Would someone like to tell me what's going on? What is a detective doing here? Don't tell me they're harassing you about Crystal's death."

"Cedric, please, I'm sorry, all right. I didn't want to say anything earlier, but I guess I have to now. This isn't about Crystal. Last night, Malcolm was in a horrible car accident on his way home, and his body was ejected from the vehicle. He, um, he didn't make it."

"What?" He took a few steps backward and looked as if he were going to pass out. "This is some type of joke, right? You're trying to tell me that my wife, and now my best friend, too, is gone?"

"I'm sorry, sir. I didn't know about your wife. My condolences to you. And, Mrs. Carter, I can come back later if that works better."

"Uh, no, I really want to get this over with as quickly as possible, and whatever you have to ask can be done in front of them," I said, making Cedric sit beside me. But then, I looked over and noticed Eva sitting there as quiet as a mouse. I decided not to have her leave because Malcolm had gone to her house last to be with her and the baby, so I figured she could say something that might be helpful.

"All right, if you insist." He started with his questioning. "So, you said last night that your husband had no enemies?"

"No, not that I'm aware of. He's—or he was, a very established attorney, and his family name is very well known, so I'm sure some people were jealous of him, but I don't think to the point of killing him."

"And you said everything in your marriage was fine?"

"Yes, sir. Like I said, we had our share of problems, but I loved my husband, and I know he loved me."

"And what about you, ma'am? How was your relationship with Mr. Carter?" he asked, looking over at Eva. She stared back at him as if she'd been caught red-handed with her hand in the cookie jar.

"Me? What do I have to do with anything? You're here to question Mariah, right?"

"Well, you're here, and you *are* the mother of his child, correct?"

"Yes, I am—his only child. And I never would have done anything to Malcolm. There's no way I would have left my child without a father."

He put his head down and began writing in his little notepad before continuing.

"Can you tell me where your husband may have been coming from, Mrs. Carter?"

"Um, as far as I know, Eva's home. He left here with her to make sure she and the baby got home safely."

"Really? And how old is Mr. Carter's son?"

"He's one month old, Detective."

"I see," was all he said.

"Wait, you see *what?*" Eva asked angrily.

"You know what? That's all the questions I have right now. But if we discover anything more, or I have any other questions, I will definitely be back in touch with you, all right?"

"Oh, um, sure, of course. Well, let me walk you to the door."

We got up and headed toward the door, with Cedric coming with us. The minute we were there, he offered his condolences to Cedric and me once again before leaving. Then I turned to Cedric.

"I'm going to get out of here too, Mariah. I'm sorry, but I just can't be here right now."

"Trust me, I understand. I barely want to be in this house myself right now."

We hugged long and tight before he released me and whispered, "Mariah, promise me you'll be careful with that woman. There's something about her that's just not right. I was going to talk to Malcolm about it, but now, well, you know. But please, keep your eye on that woman, all right?"

"Okay." I nodded as he kissed my cheek and walked out the door. Then, I turned around and headed back into the living room.

Eva started to go right in. "Did you hear him? Who the hell did he think he was?"

"What? What are you talking about, Eva?"

"That damn Detective Morris or whatever his name is."

"It's Murphy, and again, what are you talking about? The man was only doing his job by trying to help find out who killed my husband. Don't you want to find out?"

"I do, Mariah, but open your eyes. He's trying to accuse me, and I won't let that happen."

"Eva, I don't think he tried to accuse you any more than he did me. He was only doing his job."

"Yeah, well, he's barking up the wrong damn tree, and if he knows what's good for him, he won't ever think about questioning me again."

"What do you mean, 'if he knows what's good for him'?"

"C'mon, Mariah, it was only a figure of speech."

The room became oddly quiet before she brought up something I never imagined her to be concerned about.

"So, um, your friend, though, Cedric. He said that something happened to his wife?" she asked, following me into the kitchen.

"Um, yes, my best friend, Crystal. There was some type of accident at her home last night."

"Really? Wow, on the same night of Malcolm's death. That's crazy."

"Yeah, it is," was all I could say.

"And have the police discovered anything? Like what happened, or who did it?"

"Who did what, Eva?"

"What?" She gazed at me with two big puppy-dog, innocent-looking eyes.

"Who did what? I only said there was some type of accident. That's it."

"Oh well, I just figured that meant like a murder-type of accident. That's all."

"I see," I said, looking at her odd behavior that went right along with the words from her mouth. Then it dawned on me. "Crystal, where's MJ?"

"Um, home. I left him with my neighbor so I could come here with you."

"Well, you know what? I think he might need you a bit more than I do right now. And plus, I need to get dressed and connect with Malcolm's friends and family."

"Oh, okay. Um, sure. But I had one quick question before I left. Have you found Malcolm's will?"

"Eva, why are you asking me anything about my husband's will?"

"I just thought that it would be best to have his will with the funeral arrangements as well as dividing things up between you and MJ, of course."

"Yeah, of course," I said, thinking about what Cedric had said right before he left. "Well, don't you worry your little head about Malcolm's will or what MJ has coming his way. I will make sure my husband's son gets exactly what he has coming to him. Now, if you don't mind."

"Sure." She cracked a fake smile as we walked to the door, and then she turned around to face me again. "Mariah, I know that we didn't come into each other's lives on the best of terms, and I'm positive that there still might be a little bit of animosity between us, but I'm hoping this tragedy brings you and me closer together. I really want the three of us to be one little family. And I hope you know that I will be here for you every step of the way from here on out."

With that said, she finally left, but it was her last words that scared me the most . . . *she planned on being here every step of the way.*

Chapter 41

Mariah

It had been three and a half weeks since Malcolm's and Crystal's deaths, and I was still just as torn up inside as the day it happened. Getting through their funerals had been the toughest thing I'd ever had to deal with in life, other than when my brother passed away. Cedric had Crystal's funeral first. It was small and intimate, and he only had their families and closest friends. The authorities were still working on her case too. The only thing they had come up with was that whoever it was must have known she would be home alone. And for some strange reason, they felt the attacker was a woman, but other than that, they hadn't gotten much further.

I had Malcolm's service the week after hers. It was like a repeat of raw emotions all over again, but on a much larger scale. Everyone who was anyone had come out, whether they knew him personally or not, simply because his name was Carter.

That day, I didn't have much time to grieve from having to hug and shake hands with most of the attendees there. In fact, my grieving came once I'd gotten home by myself. I think I shed every tear I had inside of me, but that wasn't enough. I missed my husband dearly every single day and didn't think that was a feeling that would ever go away.

Cedric, of course, was just as crushed as I was over Malcolm's death. He mainly kept to himself and was extremely quiet on the day of his service. I didn't hear him say more than a few words to anyone unless he spoke to me, Malcolm's parents, or CJ. Other than that, he was mute and even decided not to attend the repast.

The only one who seemed fine and upbeat was Eva. I didn't see her shed one single tear the entire day, and she almost walked around like a queen on a throne. She made her way to speak to everyone there, announcing herself as the mother of Malcolm's only child. It was sickening to see, so much so that his parents said they would never accept her. I was just glad that I hadn't seen her all day.

Ever since his service, she'd made her way by the house daily. She claimed she always came by to check on me, but my gut told me something completely different. Not to mention the fact that she always found a way to bring up Malcolm's estate or ask for money for MJ needing this or that. It was all beginning to be a headache that I was glad I didn't have to deal with tonight.

The bell rang as I got ready to curl up on the living room sofa with a bowl of popcorn and glass of wine to watch a movie.

"Oh Lord, please, don't let this be Eva," I said while walking to the door. But to my surprise, it was Cedric.

"Cedric, I didn't know you were planning on coming over tonight. Is everything all right?" I asked, noticing the look on his face.

"Uh, I need to talk to you about something. Do you have a few minutes?"

"Of course I do. Come on in." I hugged him as he entered and walked into the living room. "What's up? How have you been?"

"I don't know. Just taking things day by day, you know."

"Yeah, I know. Same here. I just think it's crazy that we're both going through this at the same time."

"Me too. But, Mariah, I came by because I had to talk to you about something."

"It sounds serious. What's going on?"

Without saying anything, he handed me a little pink book with a lock.

"It's Crystal's journal. I hated reading her private thoughts, Mariah, because even with her gone, I felt I was invading her privacy. But I needed to have a part of her near me and feel close to her again. Now, I wish I could take it back."

"Really? What did she say?"

"Mariah, Crystal didn't love me. At least, not the way I thought, and from the looks of it, I'm not sure if she ever did."

"Cedric, that's crazy. What do you mean Crystal didn't love you? You were her husband, and you two have a beautiful little boy together. And you've been together since high school, so what are you talking about?"

"Well, she chose me because she couldn't have the man she was truly in love with."

"I don't understand, Cedric. Crystal never talked to me about any other man."

"I think that's probably because she couldn't. The other man was Malcolm. She seemed to have been in love with him since we were kids, and since he didn't want to be with her, she chose to be with me."

"Malcolm? No, that can't be, Cedric. Are you really trying to tell me that my best friend and your wife was in love with my husband?"

"Yes, that's *exactly* what I'm saying. And not only that, but also CJ is not my son. He's Malcolm's."

"All right, now, I know that's *not* true. You must have read more into her words than what she said. My best friend could not have had a baby by my husband. That's insane," I yelled at him for even saying it.

"Mariah, don't you think I feel the same way? I'm just as pissed and confused and as furious as you are, but the truth is right there in our faces in black and white. And whether or not we like it, we have to deal with it, so that's what I'm trying to do."

"I refuse to believe this, Cedric. I refuse to believe that the man I loved more than life itself and my best friend, who I shared practically all my secrets with, share a child together. Especially when she knew I could never give him one."

"I understand." He wrapped his arms around me and held me tight. "But it's true. My son is my best friend's child, and my wife never planned to tell me. I just figured that maybe that's why she'd written it all down. Maybe she hoped that one day I would find her journal and discover the truth that she just couldn't seem to say."

"So, now what? What are you going to do when it comes to CJ?"

"Mariah, it doesn't change how much I love that little boy. He is mine whether it's by blood or not, and I will continue to raise him as such. Of course, if that's all right with you."

"Um, of course, yes. You're all that he knows, Cedric. And he's already lost his mother. He needs his father . . . you . . . more than anything."

Chapter 42

Eva

"I can't take sitting in the house anymore. We need to find a way for you to access my money without anyone finding out."

"Well, Malcolm, besides killing her off for the money, what else do you want me to do?" I asked, irritated that his money and riches had been his only focus lately.

"That's not funny, Eva. But there must be a way that we haven't thought of yet."

"Look, I have asked her repeatedly about your estate, I've questioned her about your will, and I've even put the recording device in the living room of her home. What more can we do?"

"I don't know, but I'm sick and tired of just sitting in this house day after day like—"

"Like what? Like you're *dead* or something?"

"I see you're full of jokes tonight, but I'm trying to be serious. I'm tired of sitting here, unable to communicate with the outside world, unable to work, and barely having enough cash to do anything I'm accustomed to doing. This is getting old, and I don't know how long we can keep this up."

"Wow, well, I'm sorry that life with MJ and me is so horrible for you," I said, leaving the kitchen and going toward my bedroom.

"Listen, I didn't mean that, and you know it, but I'm just saying that living a life I'm not used to is something I didn't consider."

"You mean, living a life of the less fortunate, like your son and his mother?"

"Eva, what's wrong with you? Why have you been so moody and angry lately? I would think that you would be the happiest woman alive now that you have what you want."

"Oh, and what's that, Malcolm?"

"*Me*. After all, this *is* what you wanted, right? So, what's the problem?"

"You *really* want to know what the problem is? I'll tell you what the problem is. I'm tired of you complaining that your life is so bad now, and I'm tired of talking about money and what you're accustomed to. I'm sick of entertaining your wife by going over there daily, and I'm tired of watching my back every time I make a move from being afraid that the police will arrest me at any second. Malcolm, I want my old life back."

"Well, maybe, just maybe, you should have thought about that before you begged me to leave my wife to be with you, especially before you killed her best friend."

"I don't believe you, Malcolm Carter. How *dare* you throw that in my face when everything I've done, I've done for you, *including* killing Crystal."

"What does your killing Crystal have to do with me? And you know what? If things with me are so bad, why don't we call this off right now? How about I go back to Mariah and tell her everything? Tell her I lied and faked my death just to be here with you and MJ. Is *that* what you want?"

"Is that what *you* want?" I asked right back at him, testing his words.

"Look, I can't deal with this right now. I need to focus on how to access my estate, and that's it."

"I'm sorry, but I think you mean *MJ's* estate."

With that said, he walked out of the bedroom and slammed the door shut. I was absolutely furious with him, and if he weren't already pretending to be dead, I'd kill him. Trying to calm myself down, I sat on my bed and thought about everything we'd just said. I hated admitting it, but he was right. I wanted to be with Malcolm so much that I never realized until now how very different he and I were. I was okay and knew how to live without tons and tons of money at my disposal, but that wasn't his life. He *needed* the money to live the way he always had. He *needed* it to be happy, and that just wasn't me.

A few moments later, I decided to go into the living room and talk to him, but he was sitting with a strange look when I got there.

"Malcolm, what's wrong? Are you okay?"

"No, I'm not. I turned on the recorder from the device you had left in Mariah's living room. Cedric was there, and they were holding each other, and suddenly, he kissed her, and, um, she didn't stop him. She kissed him back. That's when I turned it off."

Listening to him only confirmed what I was about to say to him. We weren't meant for each other, and as quiet as it was kept, he truly loved and needed his life back with his wife.

Chapter 43

Mariah

I couldn't wrap my mind around everything that Cedric said or what had happened while he was here. That he suggested Crystal was in love with Malcolm and that CJ was Malcolm's son was more than I could fathom. I tried so hard not to let it bother me, but the truth was, it did. And just the thought of their betrayal made me break down right in front of him. Then, before I knew it, he wrapped his arms around me, and in our comforting each other, he kissed me. And for a moment or two, I let him. It felt good to have someone's lips next to mine. That was . . . until I realized what we were doing, and I made him stop. I told him I'd always loved him as a brother and wouldn't jeopardize our relationship because we were lonely and vulnerable. Thankfully, he'd agreed, apologized for kissing me, and left.

Now, I sat on my sofa in pure silence, about to read the words of my friend from her journal that Cedric left with me. Although I already knew the truth as he told it, I needed to see it with my own eyes. I opened it up to the first page and slowly took in her words about the weekend I'd left for a business trip.

Malcolm had no idea I was coming over. I didn't even know what I was doing there myself. All I knew was that I was tired of the same old routine with Cedric, and I longed to feel Malcolm inside of me. And with Mariah being away, I thought it was the perfect time. He let me into the house, and my nose took in his scent at once. He smelled amazing, and his scent alone made me want him more than I did before I arrived. Then there were his strong, muscular features. As I gazed at his body through his clothing, I imagined his arms all around me . . .

I tried to keep reading, but my heart wouldn't let me. Reading my friend's words about my husband was far more than I could bear. *What was she thinking?* I thought. And *why would she do that to me?* I kept torturing myself, thinking about Crystal and Malcolm being together, when my doorbell rang again. This time, I was positive it was more than likely Eva, so I had already started formulating a reason for her not to stay. However, once I reached the door, I saw Detective Murphy standing there without his annoying counterpart.

"Detective Murphy," I said, opening the door and almost happy to see him. "How are you?"

"I'm well, but I think the question is, how are *you?*"

"I guess you can say I'm as good as can be expected."

"Good. But did I catch you at a bad time?"

"Um, no, not at all. Please go ahead and come in and have a seat." I walked him into the living room. "Can I get you anything to drink?"

"No, I'm fine. I'm here on official business. I wanted to talk to you about some things that I've recently discovered."

"Don't tell me you've discovered something about my husband's accident."

"Well, why don't we start here first," he said, handing me a group of photos. "Does this person look familiar to you at all?"

"Uh, I don't know. The pictures aren't the best quality, and the person is in all black, but . . . wait . . . that almost looks like . . . Eva."

"Right. That's exactly what I said."

"But, I don't understand. What's going on?"

"Well, these pictures are from a surveillance camera of the store across the street from your friend's home. It caught her on camera the night of Crystal's death, going in, and leaving later."

"Wait a minute. Are you saying what I *think* you're saying?"

"I think so, Mrs. Carter. We've found your friend's killer."

"Eva killed Crystal? Oh my God. I would have never suspected that she would be involved in this. Have you already told Cedric?"

"No, not yet. I wanted to speak to you first because that's not all the news I have for you. But for the rest, I would like you to ride with me."

"Take a ride? Where to?"

"Uh, you'll find that out in just a bit. So, are you up for it?"

"Um, okay, I guess. Just let me grab my shoes and purse."

We hopped into his truck and cruised down the expressway at a steady speed. I had no idea where we were going, but I didn't even care for some reason. It felt good to get out of the house, get some air, and be in the presence of a man. As we drove, I began to look around his truck. It was spotless inside and smelled of his cologne. I watched as he turned his station on smooth jazz, which immediately calmed my nerves from all I'd discovered during the day. And although we really didn't know much about each other, I felt very comfortable with him.

We found ourselves talking about a little bit of every-thing from life and death, careers, relationships, and sometimes, nothing at all. It simply felt good just to laugh and be free with someone. I enjoyed everything about Detective Murphy, including his handsome fea-tures. But before I could get too caught up with his good looks and charm, we pulled up to Eva's home.

"Wait a minute. Are you here to arrest her? With me in the car?" I questioned as I saw other police cars pull up and turn off their lights.

"Uh, not quite. I needed you to see something with your own eyes."

Detective Murphy got out of the truck, pulled out a bullhorn, and began to speak.

"Eva Tucker and Malcolm Carter, come out with your hands up. Your house is surrounded."

A few minutes later, I saw her and my "deceased" husband exit her home. Immediately, I got out of the truck and walked over to him. I had to get close and allow my eyes to take in every single inch of him. We stared at each other for a few minutes, not saying a word, until he finally spoke.

"Mariah, honey, I'm so sorry about all of this, but you gotta know that I never meant to hurt you. I just thought I was doing what I needed to do for my son."

Without responding, and with all the anger inside of me, I lifted my hand, hauled off, and smacked him as hard as I could.

"Please, Detective Murphy, get this piece of trash out of my sight."

The officers started to walk both of them to the cars, until Eva stopped and looked at me.

"Mariah, I know a mere apology won't fix things, so I won't bother saying I'm sorry. But I beg you to please get MJ, take him, and raise him as your own. And, please, one day, just let him know that he had a surrogate that loved him just as much as his mother."

The officers took them away, and I went inside to get MJ. Once I made it to his bed, I looked at his little face looking back at me, and I couldn't help but think back to the prayer I'd prayed to God.

"Man, God, you really have some wild sense of humor . . . and I love you. Thank you for answering my prayers."

Three Months Later . . .

Chapter 44

Mariah

Looking around my new home, I thought how incredible God truly was. The space wasn't a 24,000-square-foot mini-mansion by the water, but it was precisely what I wanted and needed. I finally had my three-bedroom, two-and-a-half-bath condo, and it was big enough for me in a quiet and beautiful community with no water around. I was happy and at peace in my spirit, and I owed it all to the man above.

It had only been three months since my ex-husband, Malcolm Carter, had faked his death, and he and his son's mother, Eva Tucker, had been charged with the crime. But in just that short time, God had shown me His power, and I was finally a true believer in Him and His miracles, signs, and wonders. Not only was I a believer, but I also became a member of my new church home, only five minutes away from my condo. It was all more than I could have ever prayed for, and I thanked God daily for His goodness.

As I finished unpacking my dishes in the kitchen, I suddenly heard someone ringing my doorbell. The second I opened the door, my face lit up with a huge smile when I saw Cedric, April, and CJ.

"Hey, you three," I said, hugging each of them.

"Hey, Mariah," Cedric greeted me. "I thought we would stop by and bring you a little housewarming gift," he said, handing me a bottle of red wine.

"Oh, Ced, you didn't have to do that, but I appreciate it. Trust me, after unpacking all these boxes, I'm sure it will come in handy later when it's time to relax."

"It looks like you're settling in pretty well," April said. She and Cedric had only been dating for about a month, and he continually said it was nothing serious, but I wasn't so sure about that. She was a lovely woman with a charming demeanor, and they made a perfect match in my eyes. And although I agreed with him that he should take things slow, I was still a huge fan of their being together. Plus, it didn't hurt that she was great with CJ. Anyone could tell he loved her too.

"Yeah, I think things are coming along pretty well, but it's all the unpacking that gets to me," I said, extending my arms to take CJ from Cedric and offering them a seat.

"Anyway, how's it been adjusting since—well, you know . . . everything?"

"He's been doing a lot better than I ever expected. Of course, I can tell from time to time that he misses his mother, but like the counselor said, it's normal, and we have to take things day by day. But I figure since he has April, my parents, you, Derrick, me, and his little brother, I think he'll be good in the end. But speaking of MJ, where is he?"

"In his room asleep, thank God. He's so busy only to be a few months old, and I would never get anything done if I didn't put him down for his daily nap," I said.

"I'm sure. I'm just glad that little boy has someone like you in his life. It's a shame that neither his mother nor father will ever be able to experience him growing up."

"Yeah, I think about that all the time, but I have decided that as he gets older, I will take him to see her if Eva is doing well. I still believe that he should know his real parents."

"You're a good one, Mariah, because after what the two of them did, I would say good riddance. He's much better off without ever knowing either one of them."

I heard exactly what Cedric was saying, and if it had been a different time in my life, I probably would have felt the same way. But the fact that I would never be able to have any children myself naturally made me somewhat compassionate toward Eva. She had birthed this wonderful being despite her foolish actions. I still wanted her to get to know him and him to know her. It was the right thing to do.

Speaking of Malcolm and Eva, once the authorities had arrested and convicted them for everything surrounding Malcolm's supposed death, they also charged Eva with Crystal's murder. The two of them were right where they belonged, both serving life sentences while I raised MJ as my own. Malcolm wasn't enthused about the idea of me raising his son without him, but he had no one to blame but himself.

The three of us laughed and talked some more before someone else rang my doorbell. I excused myself and went to the door and found Derrick standing there. Immediately, my heart skipped a beat at the mere sight of the man.

"Hey, you." I welcomed him with one open arm and CJ on my hip.

"Hey, sweetie," he said, kissing my cheek. "Hey, little fella. How are you?"

I watched as CJ smiled from ear to ear as Derrick played with him. Then we walked into the kitchen, where he greeted everyone. Although I was trying to take things slowly with Derrick, or Detective Murphy, I had to admit that he was more than I could have ever wished for in a man. True enough, he wasn't everything Malcolm was, but he was all I needed. He was handsome, hardworking, caring, sensitive, strong, intelligent, ambitious, and most of all, God-fearing. We were becoming so close in such a short time, and I could see him becoming a permanent factor in MJ's and my lives.

Looking around the kitchen, I realized that I didn't need the lavish home and cars and millions of dollars in my bank account that I had before. All I truly needed was God, His love, and to be surrounded by good people that loved me, and I loved them back. Everyone in that room had my best interests at heart, and that truly meant the world to me.

As we all laughed and talked, and I even popped open the bottle of wine Cedric and April brought, I noticed Dr. Taylor's name buzzing across the top of my cell phone. Quickly, I left the kitchen and went into another room to take her call.

"Dr. Taylor, how are you?" I answered.

"I'm great. How are you, Mariah?"

"Pretty good. I can't complain. But I suppose you're calling about scheduling my hysterectomy?" I asked after finally having the guts to tell her I was ready to have it, especially now that I had MJ in my life. I didn't want to take any chances regarding my health. That was why I'd visited her office a week ago, had some tests run, and informed her that I was ready.

"I am calling about your test results, Mariah, but it's not about scheduling your surgery."

"I don't understand. What do you mean?"

"Well, it appears that I'm going to have to keep my eye closely on you for the next six months or so . . . mom-to-be."

"What?" I screamed. "You've *got* to be kidding me."

"Nope, not at all. Mariah, you are pregnant, my dear. So, now I think I should ask, do you believe in God and miracles?"

. A flood of tears came rushing down my face as I answered her. "Yes, yes, I do. With all my heart and soul, I do."

I was so overwhelmed with the news that it didn't dawn on me until sometime after the call. This baby had a chance of being Malcolm's or Derrick's. *Oh, what a tangled web we weave.*

The End